MAN-MADE FIBRE

Author of an acclaimed first novel, *A Foreign Country*, which was shortlisted for the Whitbread First Novel Award, 1999, Francine Stock is a well-known radio and TV journalist, currently a regular presenter of BBC Radio 4's 'Front Row'. She is married, with two children, and lives in London and Hay-on-Wye.

ALSO BY FRANCINE STOCK

A Foreign Country

Francine Stock

MAN-MADE FIBRE

VINTAGE

Published by Vintage 2003

2 4 6 8 10 9 7 5 3 1

First published in Great Britain in 2002 by
Chatto & Windus

Vintage
Random House, 20 Vauxhall Bridge Road,
London SW1V 2SA

Random House Australia (Pty) Limited
20 Alfred Street, Milsons Point, Sydney
New South Wales 2061, Australia

Random House New Zealand Limited
18 Poland Road, Glenfield,
Auckland 10, New Zealand

Random House (Pty) Limited
Endulini, 5A Jubilee Road, Parktown 2193,
South Africa

The Random House Group Limited Reg. No. 954009
www.randomhouse.co.uk

A CIP catalogue record for this book
is available from the British Library

ISBN 0 099 44069 5

Papers used by Random House are natural, recyclable
products made from wood grown in sustainable forests.
The manufacturing processes conform to the environ-
mental regulations of the country of origin

Printed and bound in Great Britain by
Nørhaven Paperback, Viborg

To JeanAnne,
with love

WITH HINDSIGHT, he would not have made the call. He might have left work a little early that day. After all, it was hardly a crime. Over the years the Company would get its money's worth. In golden eggs, you might say. Arriving home, he would have sat her down at the kitchen table. Their little Formica table with splayed legs like a giraffe, and remarkable tensile strength in the joints. He would have taken her face between his hands. Then again, he could never have done that; it would simply have embarrassed them both. No, he would have looked straight into her eyes and reached across to lay a finger on her forearm, at once serious and tender. Tender, that would have been right.

The children would have been in bed, or better still nearby but distracted. They might have been playing in the garden, beyond the French windows, their squabbles diluted by the evening air. Patsy would be looking back at him and between her eyebrows there would be that little cross of concentration. She would be curious and a little impatient and a little apprehensive, too. He would sweep her along with a speech about these new plans. He'd find words and a candour he wouldn't learn for another twenty years or so. Odd, to learn to talk to your first wife from a woman who at the time in question was some three thousand miles away. Possibly even drawing up a guest list for her tenth birthday party.

He would have presented Patsy with his great adventure and, with her approval, made it theirs. By what he said, and even more by the way he looked at her, as the kids came in a curious group to breathe on the glass, he would have persuaded her of his enthusiasm, his trust and his love.

With hindsight.

1

T HE TELEPHONE stood on the desk in his office, third
floor. The green carpet, thin durable felt, stopped
short of the skirting boards by a hand's span; on the walls,
textured paper – a discreet grid of bamboo stalks; on the
rectangular desk, a blotter, its paired penholders angled
apart like antennae.

Alan's secretary understood that her boss had little time
to appreciate her efforts, but it was good to keep it tidy. A
scientific mind benefits from order. The telephone sat
square at the edge of the leather blotter, its dial polished
bright. Alan ran in, pulled the door to behind him, slipped
his jacket off, slid into the chair, kicked the casters, and
reached for the receiver. Every move broke that diligent
matrix of squares and rectangles. His secretary's nylons
dragged down from her suspenders in perfect isosceles
triangles, but he'd never know that.

The call ran along the twisted brown cable, parallel

with the edge of the carpet. The cord stretched away, tense, in imitation of the miles of fibre and yarn on the factory floor beneath him. It reached up the wall by the door, slipping out at the top corner and into the corridor, dipping out through the window and plunging to the firm's internal exchange. From there it took strength, each click of the returning dial charging the dynamo of his message. It slid along the side of the low administration block and the canteen to the square-built entrance lodge with its metal windows. By the time it was pulsing across the road, high above the works bus taking the afternoon shift across town, he was almost screaming with impatience for her to answer.

Finally, the clicking gave way to silence and the silence gurgled into a subdued, suppressed ringing tone. It rang five times – could she be out? – at lunchtime? – and then he heard the metallic clunk and, after a beat, her voice, high and formal.

Patsy's kitchen made the most of those awkward corners. Taking a cue from the understair overhang, it adopted the diagonal as its keynote. Across the chequered floor, ranks of black tiles dominated the marbled olive green. When she came into the kitchen, Patsy sometimes felt a playful swing in her step: she dodged the green, walking on the glossy black with its tiny flecks of cream. A kitchen pretty much of your own design made such a statement. She did seem to have a flair.

And the floor with its simple chequerboard contrasts provided that all-important backdrop. The kitchen was a good size, one of the strengths of these new houses. Lucky, too, that it was south-facing: the plant on the windowsill thrived, that hint of Mediterranean exuberance, framed between curtains – just strips for show; goodness, who needed curtains in a modern kitchen? – with little pots and tureens dancing on them. The olive was picked out again with bold rust in the fresco colours of the walls. Very clever pattern, that abstract mosaic, Florentine, of course – sophisticated but practical. No trace at all of Sally's disastrous flurry with the electric whisk, little sign of the wear and tear of meals for the children followed by suppers *à deux* when Alan came home. Wipe down and the laminate shakes off the dirt, its colour and character unsullied.

And it was all beginning to come together. Through the serving hatch the eye could catch the golden tones of the living area-cum-dining-room-cum-study, altogether more convivial with the new wallpaper, diagonals again, the Scandinavian influence still effective. Open-plan but divided. Efficient and yet decorative. With the duty to entertain that Alan's job would increasingly involve (a shiver of anticipation and nervousness here, despite the underfloor heating; you shouldn't tempt fate, but who could help it?) there would be fresh chances to express their style. Patsy and Alan – the Hopkinses at home.

The telephone. She froze at its intrusion which drilled

cold into the copper and gold of her living room and punctured the syrupy smell of baking. It was an important sound, a call to action. She stepped quickly to the foot of the stairs and glanced up, as if three-year-old Sally might already be standing at the painted banisters, howling protest at the interruption of her nap.

He sounded so delighted, smug even, that he'd surprised her by calling in the middle of the day. "Can't I call my wife?" he burbled, rushing over the little sigh of impatience that followed her breezy recognition. "Can't I call my wife?"

"Of course, darling. What is it?" She didn't know what made her disapprove but, unless he had something important to announce, he'd be home in a few hours. And Sally was so grouchy if she woke early.

"I'm off to America. They're sending me to America. Next week – for a month. No, not that long, I'm sure, probably less. It's the project – you know, the new fibre, the one I've been plugging away at. They're impressed in Bettesville, so Rookin says. Only one man's put that combination together and taken it to lab tests so quickly, and that's your husband. So." She heard the flourish in his voice.

"What's more," he was racing now, "they're giving me a dedicated team – just two or three, but still – and they want to do comparisons with the work that some of their best lab men are doing, have been doing for years. They're really in a hurry now. And they think what I've found might just provide some way forward. You know, I've been saying this for months now – the old firm just doesn't have the dynamism. Well, now HQ is taking an interest. Now we'll see what happens."

"The same head office," she interjected, hearing the sourness in her voice, a fierce desire to cut through his enthusiasm, "that just a few months ago bought your expertise for a few dollars, kicked the old firm over?"

"Oh, I know." His laugh was rueful. "But sweetheart, you know, this *is* something."

"Obviously." Her voice was quiet, acquiescent. She looked down at her sandals. Inside the stockings, her toes flexed.

"Well . . ." He burst into the silence, not hearing her tone. "The firm's always been respected. The good, original, work gets done here, everyone knows that. Here they do, anyway. But the progress, Patsy – I know this, even you know this – the big steps forward, all happen over there. I can have the original idea, I can do the crucial development – but they make it work. Well, let's hope they do."

"So when do you leave?"

"Oh, next week some time." He paused, apologetically. "Tuesday, perhaps."

"You're flying, I suppose?"

"Yes . . . I suppose. I think there's a flight on Tuesday morning which they . . . well, it would be convenient."

"Convenient for them, maybe. Not so convenient for

anyone else." Horrifying, a wobble in her voice and a tight hot link between throat and eyes.

He paused. "What's the matter, darling? I know it's a bit of a surprise, but it's a damn good one."

"No, not at all, or rather nothing at all. Nothing. Casserole on the stove – I'll see you at six-thirty, darling. Bye."

In the kitchen, the sunlight glanced off the white paint of the window frame. The electric hand of the clock tut-tutted to the next minute.

She wished he was dead; she wished they were all dead, horribly mutilated and silenced, thrown into feeble chaos by a random fireball that had tunnelled through the atmosphere and landed, with cruel precision, on the premises of Next Generation Textiles (Nexgen) Ltd, now a wholly owned subsidiary of Lavenirre Inc., of Delaware.

Telephone calls. You know, sometimes I think that generation, the one after mine, they've conducted all their important moments, the conversations that change things, on the phone. Is it a shame? I don't know. I suppose so: it probably was for the Hopkins.

Back then, early sixties, sixty-one or two, you didn't have to ask many people to know that Alan and Patsy Hopkins and their three blonde children had made a difference to the area. They'd moved here just a couple of years before, when Sally was a tiny baby, darker then, in a big Silver Cross pram. Her brother James, he'd rock the suspension, like an experiment. And Lucy, the elder girl, she'd be scowling in her pale-blue coat, so neat, standing on tiptoes to look into the blankets at her little rival.

Two years wasn't long – but when people had style, it was long enough to make an impact. We all lived quite close, a cul-de-sac. It wasn't cramped, of course, but sometimes you could hear things. When it was quiet, on a summer's afternoon with the windows open. A shout, maybe, or if that telephone rang. And for them it rang more than for most. Alan was very clever, of course, very clever indeed. Nobody knew quite what it was he did, but he was working on some kind of new nylon – no, that couldn't be right, how could you do that? – anyway, he was a bright young scientist in synthetics. Making new fibres that would one day do away with smelly old wool and limp cotton that went that eau de nil shade after too many washdays. Strong, too; they wouldn't pull out of shape or shrink or run, he said. Well, maybe if you were rough with them, but you had to look after clothes then, didn't you?

And Patsy – well, she was a stylish girl. So chic, wonderful blonde – ash blonde you call it, don't you? – not brassy, just cool. A light wave and cut so neatly at the nape of the neck. And always interesting earrings. Costume, of course, but clusters of stones or ceramic, striking but not brash at all. She did buy locally, of course – Alan's salary, although he was doing well, can't have been that generous – but she always had the latest look. She must have been nifty with the sewing machine to get those clothes off the magazine page and into her wardrobe so quickly.

But the thing that was impressive about the Hopkins wasn't their looks, although they were handsome enough. Alan could have passed for a film star – regular features, medium build, chestnut hair – if it wasn't for that little frown, myopia, I think. No, the thing that gave them such verve was that they worked so well as a team. She was the ideal helpmate. She was attractive, ambitious for him and, in her own way too, organized enough to give form to his life. He had other things to think about, after all. But more than that, they shared goals, they shared a sense of humour, they shared the children, too, it goes without saying, but there was another kind of force between them. They both believed in the modern. They could remember the war, they'd seen what their parents had had to cope with. They wanted something better for their own children. It's natural. With hard work and some imagination, they were going to build something better.

Ah, well.

2

A LAN HAD once said that Springfield Drive wouldn't
cut its losses. He thought it undignified the way it
clung to the inheritance of the old avenue which wound
across the meadow and up to the big house on the hill,
long demolished. Patsy countered that each of the sixty
new houses was well placed and the plots were generous.
None overlooked its neighbour. No leaded light window
opened on to anything more than an oblique reflection in
the sightless eyes of the house opposite. Each boasted its
own variation – lapped boards or tile-hung, a low-slung
dormer, French windows or racy slope of eaves. Old status
and modern convenience had spawned these three and a
bit bedroom dwellings. Nothing wrong with that, Patsy
had added. For now. We'll go truly modern next time,
when we can afford it.

Up the Drive, the wives were checking on kettles,
putting pale prepared dishes in milky Pyrex under wire

domes to protect them from the flies, sloughing off their house shoes and squeezing on the slingbacks, smoothing down the shampoo and set that had to last one day more. Electric clocks, black digits on cream plastic, second hands hopping around the face, mooned over the kitchen doorways. No time – the children would need meeting from the bus shortly, scarcely the time, five minutes maybe, a quick cup of tea – a moment or two, just a little peek at the inside of Patsy's house, and take in those little trademark touches of hers. Dash upstairs, cardigan around the shoulders, smooth down the skirt; back door open, hop between the concrete slabs set in the grass, shiver in the shadow between house and garage, if you had the luxury of a detached garage, turn out of the driveway left or right and down the hill to the cul-de-sac.

The receiver was scarcely back in its cradle before Patsy heard the first shunting snuffles and moans of Sally's journey back from sleep. She walked away from the stairs, glancing instinctively up behind her at the kitchen clock as she passed through the door. She put the kettle on the gas ring; its weight made the overhead grill bounce. The scones were already marshalled on a plate. From the twilight of the cupboard came the packets. She deployed the biscuits in a defensive circle on the plate and cut the bought cake loose from its box. A choice now: set out cups and saucers and put milk in a jug, or to be safe, check lipstick and hair and change her shoes, ready to act the casual hostess.

Upstairs, the noise from Sally's room had become a

steady growl. Patsy felt the warmth of the child's sleep as she passed the door, but resisted. Her hand shook slightly as she pulled down the strands of her fringe and plumped the backcombed crown. A dab of toilet water to freshen up. Coral lips in a feint smile for the mirror.

In the gloom of Sally's room, Patsy pulled one of the short curtains aside. The light fell on the little bed, cutting across the squares of orange and green that floated on the beige coverlet. From beneath the fabric, a pink arm was flung up on the pillow. The child's face was flushed, her hair plastered down on her forehead with sweat.

"No . . . noaaaooo . . . no . . ." Sally was a fleshy bolster of objection.

"Come along, darling. Up you get. What a long sleep!" Patsy tried to keep her voice soft and coaxing. "Have a big stretch now."

"No." The syllable tore from Sally's body as she turned to the wall. Patsy's hand reached, comfortingly, for the child's shoulder. A throaty wail cut across her gesture. "Don't want to. No." Sally spat the phrases.

"Now look, darling. Mummy's got some guests arriving in a minute. You know, Mrs Hollings and Marie's mummy and a couple of others. You need to be a good girl now, and help Mummy with the tea. Will you do that?"

The child's dark eyes had fixed on the wallpaper. Then her face filled with scarlet rage, her eyes disappeared into the folds of her brows, and she began to roar.

"Sally, stop that. Now." Patsy thought she could hear

the seagull echo of a greeting outside. One of the women, already. "Get up, please."

"No. I won't. Don't want to."

Patsy sighed. "Get up. Now." She wrapped her cool fingers around the child's elbow and pulled gently.

"No, no, no, no, no, no . . ." shouted the child, wrestling her arm away with sudden certainty.

"Yes," insisted her mother, widening the span of her hand to hook around Sally's waist and drag her across the bed. "Now. Get up, will you?"

Sally squirmed and fought, concentrated now in her opposition. Her chubby legs thrashed at the coverlet, crushing the soft toys, morose mouse and bright-eyed millipede.

A crawling agitation ran along Patsy's arms, like an itch. It reached up into her jaw and down along her thighs. "Oh, no you don't," she exhaled, rolling the child from the low bed and on to the chenille rug, straddling the little body with her knees, pinning the heaving shoulders with the heels of her hands. Sally looked up at her, wide-eyed and alert, her curls splayed against the pretty maids all in a row. Now what?

"I want you up, now. We'll wash your face. No more of this nonsense. I've got a great deal to do – and then we can have some cake, all right?"

Sally's gaze didn't waver. Not right at all.

Patsy took a deep breath, conscious now that the strap of her dress had slid down her shoulder and her brassiere was showing above the frill of the scooped neckline. She could feel the fabric across her hips squeak with the strain.

"Oh for heavens' sake, they'll be here in a minute. Sally, if you don't get up like a good girl now, Mummy will have to shut you in your room with the curtains drawn and say that you're ill when the ladies come. Like Tom Kitten. You wouldn't want that, would you? Now, by the time I count three I want you to get up. And stop crying. One . . . two . . . Sally, please for the last time, I'm warning you – I'll have to lock the door . . . two . . . I will, you know . . ."

"No – Mummy." The face crumpled, horrified. "Mummeeeeeee."

Patsy relaxed back on to her haunches, hoisting up her dress strap. She eased away from the child carefully. Vindicated. Ashamed. "Oh Sally, come along, sweetheart. We really have to hurry now. Come on. Help Mummy."

The little girl clung on to her hand down the stairs. As they crossed the small hall, the doorbell rang and a head bobbed in the front door's diamond of distorted glass. Yoo-hoo.

The women called themselves girls but aspired to the costume and pearls of their mothers. Morning, noon and night they had no time for all the things wives were scheduled to do. Coffee mornings once a week maybe, voluntary activities perhaps – there was always someone who needed help, but most of them were fully stretched with husband and children. No one could imagine, although they could all remember, quite how their mothers managed with no washing machine or electricity, no toasters or fridges. And television, a religious dose at the twist of a knob, was just wonderful for the children; it broadened their horizons so.

Patsy was in a class of her own, of course. Patsy was something of a trailblazer. With that bone structure she could have been a model, surely; she was such a stylish girl. Everything about the Hopkins' life was contemporary and streamlined. Even Alan, not an old stick-in-the-mud at all. Not like Derek, or Michael or Keith, bless them. And so clever. And doing well. A national tonic, like the Duke of Edinburgh.

My dear, they said as she opened the door. My dear, just popping in for a minute, really can't stop, and they settled themselves around the Ercol veneer, powdered faces upturned for tea, tips, something sweet, approval.

It was up to Patsy. She stood at the head of the table, a coral-tipped hand on the teapot, feeling its heat, shivery despite the sun outside. Sally had climbed on to the widest lap and was balanced again, a peaches and cream toddler with her eye on the sponge.

The talk swirled around Patsy, the hostess. Gradually, experimentally, they ventured comments and questions. What a wonderful shade of blue – cobalt or cornflower? So clever, those little alcoves on either side of the fireplace, and the plants, and those interesting ceramics and, well, the brickwork just exposed like that. Why couldn't they think of these things?

And, of course, as ever, there was nothing to it. Just trying a few ideas, change it all around again next week.

Just something she'd seen, *Good Housekeeping*, Leslie Caron's house in Chelsea, so chic. She seemed more distant than usual, they thought, distracted, not quite her sparkling self.

Mandy Martin twisted a cigarette into a cream holder, to Sally's fascination. With her free hand Mandy pinched the child softly under her chin and winked. Mandy was Aunt Mandy, dark and buxom, cropped curls and broad haunches, jewellery on the large side too, that bit younger and smarter and bolder than the other neighbours. Not a real aunt, of course, something to do with Daddy's work. Russell to Patsy's Monroe, joked Alan, although in the same breath he conceded Patsy was probably more Novak. In front of the others, Patsy and Mandy never spoke directly of the Company and what they learnt from their husbands. It wasn't so much that they feared they might let slip sensitive information – there were three hundred local employees, after all – but rather that this discretion preserved their alliance against the rest. "You're a revelation, Patsy," Mandy had said once. "You seem so charming, so polite – but underneath, the things you say, the things you notice . . ." And they had laughed at the conspiracy, knowing the charge was only relative.

Outside, the sun was strong, bleaching the pink roses to white against the gloom of the young cypress hedge. Inside, the women chattered in the glow the sunlight gave to the round print on the orange curtains.

As the women left, Patsy saw Evie across the close. Evie was bringing in her washing, folded into a bag two thirds her size. The older woman waved firmly as if in a play, her heavy-lidded eyes creased with some joke, her purple-grey bob framing plump cheeks. Her heels clacked on the floor of the porch and into the house. The door shut neatly behind her.

Evie and Donald's front lawn was mowed in an eccentric curve, like a giant cedilla. Evie was French-born – small, forceful ugly-elegant French. Their two-tone Rover gleamed fat in the drive. Freshly painted coach-lamps hung from the porch. At the windows, the curtains were tied back in satin bunches. In the early evening, after the first gin in a cut-glass tumbler, Donald would play the grand piano in the drawing room, where others had lounges. But that was more than three hours away. For now Donald was still napping, after a morning of his part-time post-retirement job. It was the time when Evie bustled efficiently, her carmine frog mouth pursed with concentration, cutting flowers, yanking weeds, cleaning windows, pressing flannel and linen and Viyella, investing every action with slightly comic determination.

When Patsy re-emerged from her own front door, Evie was on her knees pulling a wayward clump of grass from a crack in the concrete driveway. A bandana had appeared around her head, matching navy cropped pants. Carmine varnished toes curled to the ends of her mules.

"All right, darling?" she called, without looking up.

Patsy pulled her cardigan around her shoulders and

adjusted the scarf she had thrown over her hair. "Yes, thank you, Evie," she said, "and you?"

"Oh, we're fine, darling. Fine. You had a little delegation this afternoon? Exciting for you, I expect." She swore, in French, at the weed and stabbed at it with the little garden fork. Her native language, not spoken much since childhood, emerged only for emphasis. Patsy smiled along. "Very exciting, thank you, Evie. And disorganizing. Excuse me, I do have to dash – it's school time."

Evie looked up, squinting in the afternoon sun. "Leave the little one with me, if it's easier. It's no trouble. What do you think, Sally? Shall we look for the fish in the pond?"

The child looked sideways up at her mother. She was still inclined to cling after their earlier drama but the cool green grotto in Evie's back garden was entrancing. "Come on, darling, we'll go to find the stone lady too, shall we?" The child swung shyly to Evie's side.

"Are you sure?" Patsy looked at her bracelet watch. "This afternoon has been crazy. Alan phoned from work. He has to go away next week. To America. For a few weeks, I think. It hasn't quite sunk in." She laughed a little.

"Ah," said Evie, "Then you *will* be very busy. Off you go now, don't be late."

At the school gates, the other mothers shifted position on Patsy's arrival to note what she was wearing. Spotted shift, wide cinch belt and matching pumps, translucent spotted scarf, blonde fringe worn low over her heavily defined brows, gilt earrings. She exchanged a few smiles and greetings to the usual range of flannel two-pieces and floral prints. Patsy kept one eye on the wide doorway for that moment of recognition in the children's eyes – molten pleasure veiled in nonchalance from James, Lucy's anxiety overlaid with relief.

On the way home, she found it hard to concentrate on what the children were saying. They called by the corner shop and collected a block of ice cream, Raspberry Ripple, which James carried in its bulky wrapping of newspaper, pantomiming its destruction with slurping growls and near-miss pratfalls.

That evening, when the last scrapings of custard-yellow and amethyst-pink had dried on the bowls, and the children had finally lolloped upstairs, Patsy sat opposite her husband.

Alan ate fast, with a healthy competence. Jolly nice, darling. He rarely varied the compliment. Sometimes he just smiled widely, long elbows on the table, casting the occasional glance towards the newspaper at the end of the table. After dinner, he'd read snippets out to her, if she had the time to listen; when they were first married, they used to giggle over the news together, being frugal with the lightbulb. Tonight, she saw him reluctantly dismiss the paper and take a deep breath. You can't pretend any longer, she thought, you can't act as though nothing has happened. Can you?

"So." He stretched back, legs pushing against the table

pedestal. "I'm sure that's right, not to tell them yet. Too much excitement before bedtime. Maybe in the morning. What do you think?" He didn't expect an answer, she knew. It was just Alan's way. It was so hard not to be angry.

"Do you know any more about when you're leaving? Is it still Tuesday?"

"Yes," he was suppressing the glee, averting his eyes from the shining silver vista in front of him. It was tough that she couldn't be there for this first exciting trip. She'd be disappointed, inevitably, that he would first set foot on American soil without her, but he was doing this for all of them.

"Right. So I'll put the Thompsons and the Fleetwoods off for Saturday, postpone the school fête —"

"Terrible, isn't it?" he grinned. "Sorry, darling. Sorry. Oops." The creases down his cheeks had appeared not long after his thirtieth birthday. Everyone remarked on Alan's smile, especially older women. *He's so lovely.* Oddly, Patsy had noted that the expression was increasingly confined to these deeper lines around his mouth; it didn't often travel to the eyes. Maybe it was different when he smiled at other people. Only she seemed to glimpse iron behind the affability; everyone else was impressed by Alan's new confidence and urbanity, as he emerged from the chrysalis of being a "scientist". He was physically more substantial too, less gawky, as if he was growing into that jaw. Middle age was going to suit him. It should have given her pleasure and pride, but at times it made her uneasy.

"– so do I cancel the week in Cornwall, abandon summer holidays altogether?"

"Oh, come on, it's just a month or so. I'm sure we can arrange something else. Or you could go down on your own with the kids. Your mother would go." He tried a boyish grimace, then abandoned it. Patsy didn't like jokes about her mother.

"Thank you." She began to push the knife on her side plate, scraping stainless steel on porridgey ceramic. He had receded from her now; the table grew wider, the room larger; through its wickerwork shade, the pendant light poured down on her.

"And we can invite the Fleetwoods and Thompsons another time; they'll understand. I can't think of a better reason."

"But the chances of getting them both free again on a Saturday . . . you know what they're like. And I've planned the menus and ordered the meat . . ." she tailed off, her fury growing in inverse proportion to the weakness of her case. "Oh well, I suppose there's simply no point in trying to help, socially."

"I do appreciate it, Patsy. You know I do. You always do everything so beautifully. And you will again. It's just that events are out of my hands. I have to go – and in the long run, this trip will probably do us more good than fifty supper parties. Surely you can cancel the butcher – it's still ten days away." His efforts were pathetic.

"Oh, what's the point," she pushed away from the table. The chair legs squealed against the parquet. She reached across the table and gathered the dishes to her, wheeling around to place them in the serving hatch, gathering her indignation about her like a stole.

Her almost handsome husband sighed, running a hand through his hair, returning protectively to the first thinning strands at the temple. As she walked past him into the little hall and through to the kitchen, he studied the veneer of the table, following its rivulets down to some great estuary beyond the drop-leaf.

After a minute or two, he got up and stood in the kitchen doorway, watching her back as she washed up in the flat kitchen light. Waves of soapy water crashed against the draining board.

"Do you want a hand?"

"No, it's fine. You get on with your preparation." She didn't look round.

He laughed. "Oh Patsy, what's the matter? Why are you sad?" He moved over to her and placed his arm around the small of her back, just above the frilly apron tie.

"I'm not sad," she forced the little mop into the neck of a milk bottle and struggled to extract it, smiling at her own frustration. "I'm just . . ." blowing upwards to get the fringe out of her eyes. "Go away, let me get on with this."

He placed a kiss carefully on her cheek, just below the beauty spot. "If that's what you want, poppet . . ."

Alan found his place in the study corner of the L-shaped room, corralled with light wood shelves and sheltered by the two orange lampshades on long flexes that cast their glow just above his head. He lit his pipe and pulled from his briefcase a small sheaf of papers. Paragraphs of text alternated with formulae and diagrams like honeycomb, linking and seductive, drawing him into their mysteries, tempting his fingers to reach for the pencil and make that extra connection, that bridge between the achieved, the concrete, the material that lay on the laboratory bench or the kitchen table or the bathroom floor, whose properties were listed and quantified, and the as yet unknown formula which might feel like a baby's skin or an alligator's hide, with the imaginative possibilities of both – the stuff of dreams.

3

O N THE roof of the airport terminal they grimaced into the noise. Sally had her fingers in her ears; the wind had drained the colour from her cheeks to the same cream as her sweater, leaving only red-tipped nose and red-rimmed eyes. James was leaning over the barrier, humming beneath the roar and swinging one leg between the bars, swivelling around to watch the little service trucks dart across the tarmac. A promontory stuck out from the terminal with arms extending to half a dozen planes on each side. James's eyes returned to the third plane on the right. He had been the first to identify the aircraft his father must be on. He willed it to do something extraordinary, to snatch away from its station and rampage along the runway with guttural revvings, before taking to the skies in a triumphant blast of flame and smoke that would scorch a track across the terminal roof. And he feared it too. Lucy stood beside her mother, chewing her nails, not quite touching, until she felt the warmth of Patsy's gloves on her shoulders.

Further along the terrace, the radar of the Control Tower oscillated behind the head of Fred Rookin, Nexgen's employee relations manager. He chatted and smoked with a younger man, his assistant and driver for today, their words unheard by the family in the rush of air and engine noise. The wind whipped strands of hair into eyes, leaving them shiny and stinging, but Rookin's coiffure held steady, swept over with Brylcreem, unnaturally dark.

In the departure lounge they had stood in a circle around Alan. The young man Jon, Rookin's assistant, was deputed to check baggage and seating and arrange cups of tea in the little cafeteria. Lucy gazed with aching throat at her father while James exchanged casual grown-up observations on the mechanics of air travel. After you leave us, Dad, you'll go through that doorway there and then on down that passageway. I'm not sure if you turn to left or right, but pretty soon you'll go into that tube thing that takes you into the plane. And that's your luggage, well it must be really, that they're taking out now. And the fuel goes in at the front there. The propellers on the Comet, they're fifteen foot across. Dad. Dad, they're fifteen foot across.

Sally was in her father's arms.

Fred Rookin stressed again the care that the Company would take of them in Alan's absence. He'd already complimented Patsy on her suit, the match of trim and pillbox hat, and bought toffees for the children.

"It's very good of you, Mr Rookin – Fred, sir," Alan attempted to balance gratitude with the structured informality of the American hierarchy.

"Well, I'll leave you guys alone for a while. Say your goodbyes. Have some time to yourselves – just family." Rookin smiled down at his hands and backed away out of the group. He was a large man and his absence left them more crescent than circle.

"Daddy," asked Lucy, "why does he speak like an American?"

Both parents shushed her, Patsy's challenge meeting only embarrassment in Alan's eyes.

"Well, he doesn't exactly," murmured Alan to his daughter, "but he does deal with a great number of Americans at work and that's the way they all speak."

"I like it. 'You guys.' You guys." James swaggered. "It's modern, Lucy Locket, you just don't get it, baby. Baby," he added fiercely, with the certainty of knowing how to behave if an American were there. Jimmy knows from television that all Americans are film stars or special agents.

"I do, I do – but I *don't* like it." For the eleventh time that morning, Lucy was on the point of tears.

"Hey, you two," said their father, "I'll have to go soon. Don't let's squabble." He looked at Patsy. "I will telephone when I get there, as soon it's the right time of day. Some time tomorrow afternoon, I don't know when exactly. I have to change planes in New York but it's not far to

Philadelphia and then there may be a drive, of course, but you know, big cars, big roads, it won't take long."

She smiled tightly, nodding agreement.

"I don't know how often I'll be able to call," he added, suddenly anxious. "But I'll write, children, I'll tell you all about it. All the funny strange things – and the food, hot dogs and steaks and fudge sundaes. Although there may not be time for those." He laughed. The children nodded, solemn and incredulous.

The hollow ping of the Tannoy launched the departure announcement. Alan gathered his briefcase and news-paper, Lucy's card, Sally's drawing and James's Corgi Aston Martin. "I'll keep these with me at all times," he said with mock seriousness. "Very important."

No one spoke. The children looked terrified. To his surprise and gratification, Patsy appeared to be fighting tears. "Oh," he said, putting an arm around her shoulders and squeezing firmly, "now, now," reassured by the need to be reassuring. "No need for that. Look at Mummy, isn't she a silly girl?"

Lucy's lip was trembling again. James stared at his shoes. Then Sally gave a deep wheezy laugh and they all joined in, relieved. Silly Mummy – silly, silly Mummy.

The departure gate, dull cream with red lettering, had taken on a sinister leer. He had stood there for a couple of seconds, almost filling the frame, slightly hunched with the effort of holding the children's gifts and his bags. Then he looked to one side and was gone. There was nothing she could do, no way she could summon him back. There was only a hole, not yet a wound but strange and shocking, into which she might fall and lose everything.

She would not cry, here, in front of the children, just a few yards from Alan's superior. Intercontinental travel and spells apart – these were opportunities. We'll manage, it's fine, not so long after all. Yes, it is very exciting.

She was saving for herself a private time, when the children were in bed and no sensible person would telephone, to feel the lack of him. In the dark, warmed by tears, she could open up and rage against his eagerness to give himself over to the Company. He had left her, left her with the children and the house, responsible for everything from gas bills to wills because the great giant in Bettesville had growled a command.

Did that make sense? Don't be so silly. It made no sense. She knew that it was a good job, and a good move within a good job. She wanted him to demonstrate his skill as a research chemist, the skill that hadn't come cheap in effort. Until he had called with the news, however, she hadn't begun to realize what his absence would mean. Yet the trip led to what she wanted, what they planned for. Only now did she start to feel the desolation. It was worse for its subtlety, the way it slipped in like this, reaching its fingers in to take hold, to clutch and freeze her.

The plane hurtled along the runway. The windows in the blue stripe along its middle blurred into one long howl.

Patsy turned to the children as they squinted after the dot that was disappearing into the cloud. "Well, now." She smiled. "Home. Cheer up, you lot."

In the car, Fred Rookin laid an arm along the back of the front seat as he amused the children with stories of America. The size. The extravagance. The gadgets. Next to him sat James, boy pilot, at the centre of the Humber's generous front bench. Patsy watched the trio: Rookin's thick neck, with its pockmarks; the broad cuff on his raincoat which almost obscured the back of Jimmy's tufted head; the child's ears pink with concentration; at the wheel, Jon, a little apart, slim and straight, hair tapering down to a duck's tail, clean and responsible, graceful even. The sky had cleared and in the back Patsy's sunglasses echoed the curve of her fringe. As Rookin talked, his accent shifted west. Jon swung the car east and south, past the towering grassed slopes of the Staines reservoirs with their sprinkling of sheep, grazing almost upright.

Along the High Streets they swept, past the striped awnings and electrical displays, the butchers, bakers and hairdressers dispensing the afternoon's resolute shampoos and sets. A top-hatted halibut waved from a board by a fishmongers' slab. In neon-lit hardware stores, cartoon handymen advertised sets of spanners. Dress shops whispered mellifluous names in curly italics – Isabelle, Petrina, Madame Irene – while blouses danced on nylon wires, pleading with their outstretched arms for attention, for the warm fulfillment of flesh.

Rookin was in full flow, interrupted only by his own stagey mirth at the wonder and absurdity of life across the Pond. He concentrated his efforts on his young audience. Least he could do, really, keep the youngsters entertained. Mrs Hopkins, she was bound to be feeling a little out of sorts. Transatlantic travel can be quite an undertaking for all parties if you're not used to it. Still, she seemed cool enough. Charming, gracious – a looker, too – but cool.

Behind her glasses, Patsy was locked in tight. The Humber bounced and swished over the road, jolting her arm from time to time against the leather rest on the door. Occasionally she shifted position, causing a little sigh of slip against dress, crossing her legs at the ankle, careful not to snag her stockings, but it made no difference. Nothing could shift the frozen mass inside. She had failed to reach Alan and he hadn't been able to storm through her rage and misery. Now he was gone.

The farewell at the airport had been dreadful, but she knew it could not have been any other way. Only film stars fling back their heads and kiss to the depths of their souls. The rest of us peck fondly, smoothing down jackets, straightening hair and fussing over details, one eye on the children or the time or that strange little woman over there who's staring at us – why is she staring? Do you have this, or that? Will you, my love, remember to unpack your shirts when you arrive and lay them out carefully in the drawer? Will your body wake in a strange wide bed to recall that today it must carry a suit freshly pressed by the hotel's housekeeping? Have the eyes that might gaze into mine scanned instead the bills to be paid while you're away?

Like her, Alan had ignored her anger until it became invisible. All that remained was a transparent screen that silenced her pleas that he should not, must not, go until he knew, until they both knew — what? Loved? Needed? I, you. You, me. Some absolute indissoluble pact not signed, a leap across a chasm not attempted. Patsy could not easily forgive herself, or Alan, for that.

It was a cheat, this absence. In the old days they always planned their projects together. They had done since that first meeting. There was coral crepe paper around the central light in the university hall, when she and her friend came up from the town, pinned up and squeezed into that summer's peasant look, Anna Magnani eyes applied shakily in the cloakroom; he and his friend were loafing at the doorway, playing around, displaying. She'd not met a student before, and this student was studying not just for one degree, but planning more, and with a sports car, too — a real convertible, a little leaky and unreliable but with intention and ambition as gleaming as the rust-spotted chrome. It felt right; she was buoyed along by his enthusiasm and interest. He knew so much and he always wanted to know more — even if, at that first meeting, and in fact the second, he occasionally forgot her name. Boys she knew didn't do that: they weren't so intent and disinterested all at the same time. Once he failed to turn up altogether for a date; he'd become so involved in a practical at the lab that their arrangement slipped his mind. That would have been the end for anyone else, but he was so unforced in his apologies, so unapologetic, that he made her see the joke.

The reaction when they met was catalytic, he would pun later. An uncontrolled experiment. Somehow he always made it sound more dramatic, more unstoppable, than she could recall. Seated in the MG's bucket seat, she had sniffed bohemia in the old leather. Small matter that they drove only from campus to her parents' terraced house to the cinema. He was her redbrick lieutenant and they would plan a campaign together. He would spring her from her terraced prison.

He'd been to grammar school. His parents had a dining room. His sister's husband was a doctor. His father travelled up to London on the train each day to work in an insurance company. The first time she went to lunch there, his mother started a conversation about Mr Gaitskell and everyone joined in, except Patsy, of course. She sat there, at a loss, next to Alan's father who was kind enough. He made little jokes and she smiled back, using what she could to make him feel her gratitude, trying to fan this little conversation into life.

Alan's parents were quietly appreciative of their boy, only the second in the family to go to university. The first was an uncle who'd been killed in the war.

She was nervous of Alan coming to her home. Her mother might try too hard to impress him, embarrass her daughter by revealing that Patsy had told her things that she knew would be pleasing. Don't let on, please Mum, that I've told you about his house, or his sister or anything.

And where exactly, her mother had enquired on Alan's first visit, is your brother-in-law's medical practice? I gather your mother is from Norfolk, originally. We have family in East Anglia, in Ipswich. What was her maiden name? Mummy, we've got to go, said Patsy, the film starts in half an hour and there might be a queue. He didn't seem to notice the size of the rooms (very cosy, he'd said, and meant it). He wasn't cramped by the tiny sitting room. He didn't trip over the grand curtain into the hallway, which wasn't really a hallway at all, but a pretence that the door didn't open straight off the street. He admired the gilded mirror by the door and peered carefully at the old photograph on the table beneath it. Magnificent house, her mother had said with a sigh, as if she'd spent her childhood on its clean-shaven lawns. This mirror, just one of the many beautiful things from that house. The family always had beautiful things. And how many times, thought Patsy, did you visit those cousins?

There's nothing wrong with your mother, he'd said when they finally left for the cinema, she's charming and lively. Very well preserved, too. I see where you get your looks. And she's obviously proud of you. He was so genially casual about the house and her mother; he never could understand why her stomach knotted as she turned into the road; he never caught the ultrasonic pleas and warnings. I've made a mess of it, darling: don't do what I did. You can do better. Don't waste yourself – you can look really lovely, when you try. Don't let me down, poppet. Come here, let me straighten your seams.

For heaven's sake, Mummy, Patsy had said, you married a man with a bad heart. It was an accident, not your fault. Daddy didn't mean to go. The pension's not bad. We manage. Don't get me started, darling, her mother had said. Best not to know. But you're so much cleverer – and more beautiful – than your old mummy. You could go anywhere, with the right man.

Just across town was far enough to begin with. The sense of liberation she felt on her marriage blended satisfactorily with filial duty. Step one: out of the house. Step two: a life of their own making, a life that would exceed her mother's dreams (oh yes, please), planned by her and Alan in their joint enterprise. That was the extraordinary thing about Alan: he had confidence that things could be done. He wasn't flash or cocky, he didn't ooze charm, but he did find ways to get things done.

The job offer from Nexgen (research officer, textiles) came in the first year of their married life, as hoped, expediting the progress of sperm to egg. Jimmy was born when the last coat of paint was still tacky in their rented home in the new town. His birth triggered an extended stay by Patsy's mother, an experience not repeated with the two later children. It was all too difficult, the two of them together: nothing was ever done quite right, for either of them. Patsy didn't like to be reminded of the angry order of her mother's terraced house and was infuriated by the squadrons of Jeyes' fluid bottles her mother drilled in her own. The baby had no preconceptions; he blinked at her with soft mushroom-coloured eyes. He saw her only in that instant, no history, no ambition as yet, and he needed her.

With Alan's help, she was becoming the woman she wanted to be, free to plan a future of mushroom, mustard and cream (curtains, with little springboard designs) or red, grey and ochre in repeating columns, like Alan's lists of data. Cerise and lime were just around the corner, great swirls and splodges marching in rows. She smiled at the memory now.

She'd get over this shakiness that had ambushed her in the back of Mr Rookin's car. It would get better soon. They'd be back on an even keel. Modern marriage – her lists and organization, her strategic planning, her vision of their home and future, his execution of these shared goals in the outside world – that was the contract and they would carry it out. Their future was the expression of love. This upset phase was just that, it would pass, a time of the month, of the year, of life.

When she got back, she'd rearrange the living room – it usually worked – if there was only some way to bring the hearth into the centre of the room. She'd seen a photograph in *Ideal Home*, the layout almost identical to theirs. The open fire was set behind a sliding glass door in a promontory of wall. She could do the same on the piece of supporting wall that remained from knocking through, where the chimney-breast had once been. Alan found that little pier at the inside corner of the L-shape annoying. Now she could imagine hot red in a metal box within the white plasterwork. Dramatic and sophisticated at once. And if not naked flames (all that smoke and ash) then log-effect, flickering across the parquet to the shaggy rug.

Half an hour from home Fred Rookin took the family for tea in a café, as a treat. It was a proper Italian place, with shiny machines and checked tablecloths. Fred held Patsy's chair for her as she sat down. The driver, Jon, settled the children around him at the second table. Their heads bowed inwards to hear his jokes. The two tables were drawn closer but did not touch.

Patsy folded her hands carefully on the table, measuring halfway between wrist and elbow to rest her arms on the edge, as she'd been taught. She affected nonchalance. It was fun, yes, from time to time to stop out rather than cook. Great fun. She thought of the "occasions" when she and her mother had eaten out together – birthdays, school certificate – and the satisfied air with which her mother would look around at the Coffee House panelling. It's very nice here, she would say, very pleasant. You know, I remember once, many years ago, when I was in London with a friend from the choral group, splendid days, splendid days . . . And Patsy would cringe, but be awed too at the unuttered memory of crystal and silver plate and fresh flowers. This friend, who got away, who wasn't her father, where was he now?

Sausages, chips and lemonade arrived, and for the adults tea and a few small sandwiches filled with pale thin ham and the vinegar tweed of Sandwich Spread. Patsy nibbled politely at nothing. Refuelled, the children became noisy and competitive until Jon channelled their electricity into a game involving a finger of sandwich, the menu stand and Lucy's plastic rainhat.

Did she, asked Fred Rookin, have much idea of what her husband would be doing at Bettesville? Research, of course, but with a purpose. It could lead places, he said. It meant a great deal for the Company in England that his work was so important. If it all went well, they might need his help over there for a while. She might think of the possibility of joining him, not immediately of course, but sometime down the road. If, when, that occurred, then they would be there to help in any way they could, she must understand that.

She did, but she couldn't. The plan didn't go like that. She and Alan had completed the paperwork on the house barely three years before.

First to go had been the covings and skirtings. The modern home had no room for half-hearted curves. Goodbye, cottage look. They needed space for living. It might have been a contemporary house, all mod cons, but she had next season's ideas already. Alan had groaned when she told him of her plan to knock down the wall between sitting and dining rooms. But where will I go, he asked, if I need peace and quiet. In your study area, she'd cracked back, laughing. We're not the kind for formal dinners, anyway. We'll do supper in the kitchen.

By the time dinners were back on the menu, when Alan became the senior researcher at the Company, the Scandinavian table was installed in the L-shaped room. Alan folded his long legs under the Ercol dining chairs with the laminated seats. While his wife served and volleyed to the guests, he fingered the textured surface of the polyurethane upholstery pad beneath.

And the children? he had insisted; where will they go in this living arrangement? That's the great advantage of the bedroom-cum-playroom – Lucy and James can each have their own area, we'll put plywood boxing around their beds in the room under the eaves, like little ships' cabins. They'll be self-contained there, sailing on with all their toys. He'd nodded, persuaded of this coupling of efficiency and romance.

It made no sense that he, pioneer in the laboratory, should prove Luddite in domestic arrangements. He liked the broad sweep of lawn, the bold path of crazy paving and the upturned disc filled with ugly succulents (spaceship, said James, utterly convinced of its provenance) that disguised the manhole cover. He enthused about the glass pendant in the hall that replaced the traditional light fitting. Let's have plenty of light in this house, he challenged. Light and space. Come on, Patsy.

It was raining when they reached the house. Sally was asleep, curled warm against Patsy's thigh. Lucy was in a thumb-sucking trance, while James was acting as co-driver, changing gear with the lever that protruded from the Humber's steering wheel. For a second after the engine died away no one moved, reluctant to stir from the sanctuary of the solid vehicle.

"Well," said Fred Rookin, "here we are." He looked across at Jon, who smiled at James and swung his car door open. Rookin pushed his own door with some effort and stretched his legs with a grimace. "Not too uncomfortable, I hope," he said over his shoulder to Patsy who was trying to prop the sleeping toddler upright.

"No, very comfortable, thank you," she said. Jon opened the door beside her. "Run in, Lucy," she added to her yawning elder daughter, as she calculated the effort to carry Sally out of the car against the handicap of a tightly tailored skirt and stiletto heels.

"Shall I take her?" asked Jon. His voice was light. It was the first time he'd spoken to her directly; she'd only heard him murmur conspiratorially to the children. He was holding the door wide, too wide perhaps, as if either she or Sally were some kind of unpredictable beast.

"Oh." She hesitated. "Yes. Please. Thank you." She turned to gather her bag and gloves. Turning back, she saw his eyes were averted, gazing across the top of the car. Just above his jawline were two crescents of flushed skin, like sideburns. Patsy's reflex was snappy. She slid her ankles together out of the car and rose to her feet, teasing a glance across his face, gaining strength and height from such studiously avoided attention. He drew back a half-inch further.

She stood for a moment in the harbour of the opened car door, her face upturned to the fine drizzle, wrinkling her nose. Less than two feet from him. Then she picked her way across the uneven path to the front porch, holding her clutch bag above her hair to protect it from the rain. Under the canopy she passed the bag to James who rummaged for keys and stretched up to place the key in the lock, with ceremony. Fred Rookin stood behind, sheltering the group.

Patsy opened the door and James and Lucy trooped in. She followed, putting her bag down on the hall table. Rookin hovered on the step.

"I'll just see you all safely home. Lights on and no problems," he said.

"Yes. Thank you," she said, walking through to the living room and hugging herself against an imagined chill. She wanted to be left with the children now.

Through the plate-glass window she saw Jon carrying Sally down the wet path. The sleeping child's head was supported in the crook of his arm. The young man looked down ahead of him, grave with concentration.

The things they get them to do, thought Patsy.

4

A LAN ADJUSTS swiftly to the time difference, not the official five-hour Greenwich discrepancy but a radical repositioning of experience and consciousness. If the black hands are still hopping steadily around the cream-faced clock in the kitchen, Alan's life is now described in great shining arcs. He has left his family waving slowly by the departure gate, the children woebegone or frantic, Patsy suddenly rather emotional – funny girl, you wouldn't think for all her crisp brightness that she could dissolve like that. The news of this trip has obviously upset her in a way he can't quite fathom. Later, of course, he'll convince himself that it was only a matter of time. If he'd only given her enough time, he would have understood her and she him. Synchronicity. Alan doesn't yet, but will in later middle age subscribe to a liberal belief that awkward behaviour will submit to sufficient investment of caring attention. He would have had only to love her out of her gloom, allow her the space to be herself, to release what would surely have turned out to be a deeper, more tenacious affection. He will express this opinion to Lucy one night many years later, after a martini or two, and will find in her snigger evidence that, despite appearances, she is still only seventeen.

For now, Alan might be riding a Comet, but in fact, less poetically it's a 707. His trajectory into the leaden Middlesex sky is touched with silver the moment he is settled into his seat. He is with the Company, but more than that he is for the first time with the great company of men on Boeings everywhere, crisscrossing the globe above its mantle of cloud, weaving with their dreams a pearly textile to protect and support mankind for the future. On his own, like this, in pursuit of work, Alan feels words disengage in his brain. His customary vocabulary expands. He replaces "would" and "could" and "provisional findings" and "housekeeping" with "can" and "do" and "executive summary" and "intercontinental" and "management pyramid". An arsenal of nouns and verbs and adjectives opens itself to him, labels for this epic world.

Taking his cue from the executive in the row in front, he removes his jacket, which the perfumed stewardess hangs behind a corrugated curtain near the cockpit. The crease in his shirtsleeve still holds the faint caramel scent of Patsy's iron and for a moment he feels disoriented, drawn back down into the lawn-edging and coffee spoons of home, the clocking in and Rich Tea of the office.

He stretches with anticipation. They have sent for him. In his briefcase are the notes for the next stage of the laboratory work. Bettesville HQ has the proposal, sent ahead, but he already knows the results. For the best part of a fortnight the little bench in the far corner of the lab held an unassuming collection of flasks and beakers. At half-hourly intervals he checked the temperature, handing the task over to the obliging caretaker at night, restraining himself from inserting the glass rod into the acid yellow solution until that final afternoon, when he could tell, from the slight precipitation at the base of the flask, that it would reward him.

Of course, it's early days, but he can allow himself a few moments of speculation, here in private, suspended. Back home, there's only one contender, the big Imperial, and he undoubtedly felt a lurch of disappointment when the firm first denied that ICI was the new purchaser. It would have been the logical step. But this, this will be far more exciting in the long run. When management revealed the American interest, rather shyly, as if they'd been caught necking on the back seat, he saw that logic too. Much of the important work on the cellulosic fibres has been British, why not buy into that expertise? Why not, indeed? It was shrewd of them to recognize original work even if it originated on splintered benches under dusty lightbulbs.

Where he's going now, the benches will be spotless, Formica, wiped down by lab assistants in crisp envelopes of nylon.

And what will they call it, his discovery, his creation? The syllables stretch out, jostling for position, reaching to bond with the polymer chains. What combination of -lon or -cron, -elle or Micro-, of -lex and -lene will his caterpillar of a formula attract? Futurelle? Microspan? He glances sideways, guiltily, at the only other passenger across the aisle in his row. Alanylene? Ridiculous. Whatever the baby is called he will love it and know he was there at its conception. Better than that, in the half-perfect sphere of the test tube, he was the only begetter.

In his briefcase there is also a schedule, a series of meetings with Tom and Ray and Jack and Harry and, further up the scale, men with Jnr and III appended. They have made much, in the initial discussions, of his scientific integrity. Hey, Alan, this is your work, all we can offer is the chance to develop it under the best conditions available on the planet. The very planet that is now spinning away beneath him. He has few illusions, he's just a young scientist, he'll have no influence in a huge corporation. All he can control is the contents of his head. But his relative powerlessness makes not an iota of difference to his euphoria. It is an exciting project and he's in on it. For the next few weeks, he will *be* it, and prove himself capable of more. If they take him into their trust, it could even mean a future outside Britain, although he hasn't discussed that yet with Patsy. But she'll be game for that, if it isn't tempting fate to imagine such success so soon.

All the same, in a few years, a few months, a great deal could change.

Nobody could say their town isn't a good place to live – comfortable house, mortgage manageable if sobering, decent schools, pleasant countryside, a theatre, cinema (when they find the time) – he can't complain. Patsy is a fantastic wife, as he always knew she would be. She can keep up OK, in fact sometimes she gets there first. He'd loved that slightly defiant look when he first saw her in the student hall, even though she'd actually been quite shy and tongue-tied when they spoke. He'd known she would be. She had looked aloof, standing out from the others with that exotic gypsy skirt, but that didn't put him off. Also, he seemed to remember she had rather sweet little feet, dutiful feet. He remembered some pal once remarking on his apparent confidence with women, ribbing him for his nerve. But your jacket reeks of ethanol or hydrochloric acid, said the friend, and your fingers have those chemical burns, what makes you think they'll say yes? It doesn't smell, he'd protested. That's just in your head and it makes sense to ask, even if you only get a fifteen per cent response. I don't suffer with my ego the way you literary boys do.

He'd been right, too, dammit. The first time he'd driven her out in the old MG for a pub lunch on a Saturday, she hadn't thought his ideas were crazy. She could see what he wanted to do, even if she didn't altogether understand the mechanics of it. Scooting back through the lanes, he'd wondered about borrowing the money for an engagement ring. He was sure she'd understand the point of that, too. Sometimes in life, you just come across people who travel at your speed.

So much about Patsy is admirable, he knows. If there'd been any point, she could have gone to university; she's easily bright enough. He couldn't ask for a better wife and he knows she's up to any challenge ahead. For heavens' sake, look what she's done to their houses. Great fun. Startling almost. He's pretty much handed the reins over there. No, family life is good, although he could do with fewer bills to pay.

Tilting into the little oval window on the plane, he looks out towards the nose. Ahead the light is bright amber. It bounces on to the aircraft wing, burning the metal soft, splaying into saffron lances that cut across his eyes. Behind him, as he twists round, his face squashed against the window, he can see the purple dusk falling, distorted through the starry fingers of ice on the pane. Let them sleep back home. He has work to do.

When he wakes, the crease in his shirtsleeve has spread to a delta of crumples. His head aches from the rumble of the engine and his stomach is curdled from the scotch, but the moon has a clear high-pitched tone, as it dances along the gleaming wing, the self-same moonlight that shines on Vermont.

At the gate, they are waiting for him, Ray and Tom, accompanied by a driver with a sign that bears the corporate emblem and his name, printed. He checks the knot on his tie and strides towards them, his briefcase swinging from his left hand and the porter with his luggage trying to keep pace.

They are fleshy men, but not fat. They are generously covered with tissue sculpted by weekends at the golf club and regular laps of the pool. Tom and Ray are both dark, with hair swept back and down, parted on the left. Alan feels the inconsequential lightness of his own hair colour, faded Anglo-Saxon.

It is strange to be on their level. He has scrutinized the city from the slope of the plane's descent, bracing himself back in his seat. From above, his gaze didn't seem broad or deep enough to encompass the span of the bridges or the shining bulk of the buildings between weaving columns of traffic. He tried to count the floors, but lost his place around twenty.

Alan is disconcerted that on the ground he cannot feel he is inside this wondrous landscape. The airport is huge, granted, and shiny, but it is still a functional place whose purpose he understands. Within a few minutes, however, he is installed in the back of a car on a seat the size of a sofa (he can almost hear Patsy's snort of disapproval, although she'd have to be a little impressed; for himself, he wonders at the welding techniques for those panels, they must be nearly five foot long) while Ray and Tom recline with their backs to the driver and spar and jest about the amount of work they all have ahead of them.

Ray does most of the talking. Ray will be Alan's guide and taskmaster, his pal, his senior, his line manager (if that's yet the jargon). Ray will circumscribe his universe, in effect. If there is a problem, Ray will find someone to solve it.

Except for those organic chemistry problems, right, Alan?

Alan squeezes out a laugh, a little late. OK, Ray. Right. And pats his briefcase, which rests reassuringly over his testicles.

In the foyer of the hotel, Alan abandons all notion of comparison. The reception desk bends away into the horizon, with at least ten uniformed functionaries bowing to the slightest whim of the guest, all smiling discreetly. He fumbles with his passport and frowns over the paper-work. Ray and Tom remove themselves to an arrangement of low leather settees and sit murmuring. They've pinched the creases in their trousers and adopted similar earnest positions, forearms resting on thighs, hands clasped.

When he has extricated himself from the battery of enquiries as to his preferences on matters he has never before encountered (Turkish, sir? Sauna in the morning?), Alan swings across the lustrous floor to his new colleagues. We're all colleagues now, Alan. That's Lavenirre Corp. for you.

Alan is exhausted and unshaven. His briefcase and its contents exercise less reassuring weight in his grasp. He has come half, maybe a third, way round the world – but he is still proud as hell that Ray and Tom, canny seals in what he takes to be double-breasted Chester Barrie, are on his team. They tell him it's late, small hours. He's grateful for the information. They tell him he's going to get some rest, a shower perhaps, and they'll call back for him around breakfast, say seven-thirty? He nods enthusiastically, fingering the great gold oblong of his room key fob.

The breakfast banquet spreads before him. The waitress has taken Alan's valiant order for ham and eggs, although his stomach tumbles at the prospect. Ray and Tom have returned with reinforcements, two older men, a lofty tanned Viking with an iron crew cut and a mournful man with sallow skin. The tall man is a senior vice-president; the second man, half a head shorter, is clearly something even more important. This second man nods at Alan and stares at him as though he might be the cause of acid reflux or a resentful liver. Floating on fatigue, Alan registers that this is Frank Farebrother, Snr, and that, despite the appearance of a mortician's assistant, he is the most senior executive he's ever encountered. The waitress seems aware of this distinction and engages the man in lugubrious banter; Alan takes the opportunity to discover what makes Farebrother's appearance sinister. In between the thinning strands of dark hair that shine gelatinously above his forehead, the man's scalp bears charcoal tattoos in lines like bacteria in a Petrie dish, or carbon reactions. Alan can almost hear Patsy's squeal (only delivered later, in private, of course) and see the children's round disbelieving eyes.

There are elaborate introductions, firm handshakes and photographs. At breakfast. Alan's body is whimpering for its bed and the familiarity of home food, but it braces itself for the pose. The photographer arrives at eight o'clock on the button, his great flashlight beaming like the rising sun on the cereal packet. The men make a quarter turn away from their conversation, one forearm resting on the table, and the most senior executive places his other arm along the back of the curved banquette where Alan is perched.

The photograph is taken. It is not the first of Alan's life, nor indeed the only image of him at work. Every year in the chill English April the firm collects the employees on the factory floor, from managing director to canteen cleaner, and encourages them to articulate cheese or sausages. This photograph, on the other hand, is the first study in tones of grey and black in which Alan is a principal actor. From now on, he will feature in photographs almost weekly, eventually even more often, with an ensemble that will range from three or four to several hundred. He will be halfway down the airline steps for the flight to the Miami convention, in oblique profile in a white coat as the second vice-president inspects the laboratory, by a flip chart in front of an impressive eighteenth-century-style table edged with senior management, or rather standing redundant behind them as they all turn away from his presentation to gaze impassively at the camera. At endless meetings Alan will feature in the line-up for the company reprise. Over the years, he will move to the foreground in these photographs, the flash-light's enquiry finding the slight weight of years on his lean face. It will be Alan then whose hand is extended first in the greeting clasp, his authority and ease that will set the tone.

This morning, though, his eyes are closed in all but one of the prints the photographer produces by lunchtime. This gives him the appearance of blissful abandon, which may not be so far off the mark. After several jumpy days of anticipation, Alan is living entirely in the moment. The sensation is aggravated by the staggered rhythms of his jet-lagged body. Nothing from throat to bowel to temple feels quite where it should be and, in the midst of this displacement, he latches on gratefully to the certainties of his new colleagues and masters.

They, in turn, are galvanized by an outside threat. Alan's research is vital to them. Has he come along in time. Boy. They don't want to rush him, they know these things can't be hurried, but they do find themselves in a very competitive situation.

Alan blinks his eyes wide and recrosses his legs with difficulty between table and banquette.

Laundry is grand, Alan, just grand. Nothing to beat the crackle of a newly starched shirt – but that's a luxury for the very rich or those with time on their hands. The modern wife doesn't want or need to spend hours doing laundry. She wants an efficient durable fabric that she can put in the washing machine and have ready for the next morning when the Boss goes back out on the road for a couple of days. Half a dozen shirts, because he may want to change before he goes out for that . . . evening seminar – with the guys in the bar. But why stop at shirts? What we need, and we know you're close, is that miracle yarn that can wash, shake off the humidity and be ready again in a couple of hours – without a sophisticated dryer, maybe just on the airer or even a line in the yard. And then, if this stuff is so resilient, maybe it won't even need regular pressing. The secret will be in the tailoring; just a cool iron to restore the crease. Hey presto!

We know this; you know this, Alan – trouble is, there are others out there who know it too. We have to get a name on it and the patent in. We've only got a few weeks.

A schedule is placed before Alan, framed by dishes of butter rolls and preserves. Alan realizes that by lunchtime he will be at his new bench and that, at this rate, the secret advantage he holds in his briefcase may not last so long, after all. His enjoyment of the moment dwindles to the dregs of coffee in the wide cup in front of him. Until now he has worried about competition in an academic sense – whether his work would be more precise and solid than that of his rivals. He's now getting a sniff of the battle to provide the world with tomorrow's materials. The company commanders haven't the time to instruct him in the art of warfare, but then there's no need. Alan isn't a warrior, he's a weapon. The Man with the Formula.

Ray calls for him at seven to go to a bar downtown and "relax" with some of the guys from marketing. Alan is a relative stranger to relaxation. Work and home – the lab and the lounge – have seemed admirable poles between which to oscillate. He will take the odd pint in the evening, but he's not clubbable. The sports car wasn't for him a packleader trophy, a signal to the young lionesses; it was just an interesting way of getting from A to B. He enjoyed the mechanics of it, rather than the glamour. He has always found large groups of men slightly puzzling in their language and rituals. Ray and Tom, and all the others who've been waiting for him here, however, are entrancing. They really do seem as excited as he is, well almost as excited. By now Alan is lightheaded from the bright fluorescent tour of his new lab and the effort of memorizing names. He would like to lie down, but bows to Ray's wisdom, at once anxious about getting enough sleep and exhilarated at the idea of going out into the broad dark streets.

The bar is two blocks away. On impulse, Ray suggests they walk. Along the sidewalk, the faces of passers-by are illuminated by the windows, the bright sherbet of department stores, the soft toffee of intimate diner booths. Alan has to pace himself: the loping stride that takes him across town to the factory each morning could easily outstrip his host.

At the door, the coat-check girl ostentatiously loops the belt of Alan's mackintosh around the hanger. Other men slip off slim knee-length coats, revealing silhouettes that taper from broad shoulders and barrel chests. They walk down the half-dozen steps into the plaid and dark wood bar, where Ray bustles into a knot of five or six standing or perching on stools.

Spread out on the bar in front of them are six coins in two slanted rows; the challenge is to rearrange them into a hexagon in just two moves. The challenger, Tom, has his hands resting lightly on the edge of the bar. Hey, says Ray, my round. He slides the coins into the position with a single movement of thumb and forefinger and sweeps the pile of bills across the counter to the barman. Tom feigns outrage but cedes central place to his colleague smoothly. They have done this before. Behind the talk, Mel Torme gives way to Tony Bennett. Dancing in the dark.

Alan frowns at the coins and at all the other structures, orders, rearrangements and obvious solutions he may be missing. He needs to get to work now, away from the enervating, nauseating richness of his new surroundings. Salt and smoke, olive and vermouth make the saliva glands pour under his tongue.

The talk is of leisure and possibilities. The frontiers of Florida – a piece of land in Boca Raton, swings and handicaps, the new Oldsmobile covertible, a joke about a young guy and the twenty-dollar treatment from the red-headed nurse at the MD's surgery, the best filet mignon this side of town, audio fidelity – although seduction is easier by tape than disc, four and a quarter hours playing time on the Sony Superscope – and the wisdom of taking out a secretary in your friend's office, ruses to get her mother out of the apartment for an evening, getting hold of tickets and shaking off the opposition.

Did I see you last weekend with a blonde? Guess not, one of those hallucinatory things. Too much imagination. Lysergic acid maybe – good enough for Cary Grant and his shrink. Tried it? What do you think? But I knew a guy did. And?

And. Alan wipes his sweating palms with a paper serviette imprinted with a cartoon woman dusting in the nude; her comical jutting breasts and wide-eyed gaze point towards an open front door in which is framed a small man in suit, tie and hat. Along the counter, other naked nubiles are caught in offices, waiting rooms, garages, courtrooms and petrol stations by little guys with expressions of amiable cunning.

For one brief, hysterical, exhausted moment Alan glimpses the doors of Springfield Drive swinging open revealing . . . nothing, of course, but housecoats and print dresses. And Patsy, with her lovely body, hardly showing the signs of three children, standing in the final door in her nightdress with an exasperated smile. Alan, for heavens' sake.

Ray moves in beside Alan at the bar. So. You like the lab, you like the team? We hope you'll be happy here, Alan.

I'm sure I will, Ray. Alan tries to prevent it, but a small hiccup escapes.

Missing home a touch, maybe? Ray's eyes are dark,

glittering with something that could be compassion, or amusement.

Alan thinks of the children, sweaty cherubs wrestling with their sheets, of the close air in the summer gloom of their bedrooms. He imagines Patsy, her thick honey hair pinned back, anointing her hands with lotion before she turns out the bedside light, her list for the morning scratched in pencil on a slip of paper, front and back doors and French windows double-locked. And then he says, his speech falling into step.

Of course, Ray. Patsy, the kids. It's the first time they'll have been without me for any length of time. I worry, naturally, but Patsy's very capable. She's a great girl, Ray, special.

Which she is, he knows. Just as he knows that, for all the fatigue and the unfamiliarity, there is nowhere else in the world he would rather be than here and now, on the eve, on the edge.

5

A LETTER HAD arrived from the fundraising foundation for the new cathedral. The children's bricks had been laid in one of the buttresses to the south-west of the nave. Thank you for your family's support in this great venture. The letter was typed on crisp paper beneath an artist's impression.

The new cathedral was already crouching like a long-necked sphinx on its landscaped hill above the town. So ugly, murmured the Sunday afternoon drivers to their passengers as they completed the loop down the High Street, around by the river with its view to the Downs. Exciting, impressive, responded the councillors and clergymen, determined to claim for their own decisions made a decade earlier. I'm sure it will be lovely *inside*, once it's finished, with the pews and drapery and everything, echoed voices in shops and on buses. But, oh dear, I'm not sure about all this modern style.

Patsy and Alan had taken the children up to the site every few weeks. They'd sponsored a brick for each child to give them a stake in the red-brown future. James was fascinated by the process and ran his fingers along the pointing, rubbing them raw on the sharp particles in the mortar. The girls preferred to peer at the model and drawings, finding more substance in the smooth toffee perfection of the balsa miniature than the muddy elevations outside.

The consecration was scheduled for the autumn. Patsy wondered if one of the children might be married there some day; she could imagine the line of the gown in the aisle, the discreet gathering of guests on either side and, towering above them, the bleached simplicity of the stone interior. At the altar, whoever it was might remember their one brick share – a note for the speeches, perhaps.

She could see the colours: oyster marble reflecting the brushed metal of the lamps; during the address they would study the blue kneelers hanging from pale wood chairs. Outside the bells would sound and the elongated gold angel would point in the wind towards the future.

Once news of Alan's trip had percolated through the Drive, Patsy received a series of visits. My dear, if I can help in any way, you just have to shout; we're all here to muck in; shall I do the meet from school? Would Lucy like to come and play? The girls would love to see her.

The women were tense with offers of casual kindness. We know just what it's like, they said, wondering at the marvel of this mysterious transatlantic trip. Men, they just drop everything and leave us to cope. Poor Patsy. They scanned her face enviously for clues.

Mandy, a company wife who knew the rules, pulled back. If they couldn't share – and how could they now? – then discreet comradeship was best. Call if you need me, she said, partly obscured by a beefy arm that proffered a tin still warm from the oven. Patsy raised her eyebrows and mugged slightly through the throng. Mandy had heard snippets from her husband that indicated "possibilities" for Alan's trip. Mandy wouldn't let her win outright, she'd rather walk away, waving.

You're mad, said Mandy when Patsy outlined to her at the school gate her plan for the new fireplace. The room looks perfect – so fresh. You can't start thinking about more alterations now. You don't need a fireplace. The heating is divine. Why do you need a "focal point"? You've just created a room that does away with all that. And the cost, Patsy. Well, maybe there's something you're not telling me about Alan's little trip, but would he want to spend more on the house, right now – if you don't mind me asking?

Oh, I've worked all that out, Patsy said, scanning the children as they milled through the door. Anyway, the holiday's as good as cancelled. I'm going to get some quotes; it's not a big job. I've found out where the flue is.

The flue? I thought you wanted flame-effect; they're so

much better. And quick. And *clean*. What on earth do you want a fire for?

Oh, I don't know, it occurred to me the other night. But it would work. I think, she added as Lucy ran to her outstretched hand, it might be wonderful.

In the centre of the natural wood windowsill stood a long-necked vase of thick glass, with swirls of smoky topaz and little bubbles. She sometimes wondered if it wasn't too vulnerable there, easily overturned, but it looked just right, poised between the sofa and the curved lawn stripes beyond. It set the room off to perfection.

Or so one of her neighbours said. A group of them were there, again. Patsy was actually wondering to herself if the vase wasn't a little obvious, now that she thought about it, when Fred Rookin rang from the office. The visitors busied themselves clattering through to the kitchen with the coffee pot and drop scones, trading compliments on her decor in stage whispers.

He was reluctant to disturb her morning, but they'd had some news wired from Bettesville and he wondered, if it wasn't inconvenient, if he couldn't call round that afternoon. To explain it to her. Nothing alarming, but he wanted to tell her in person. She needn't worry about the children being collected from school. Jon could get them in the Humber – they'd recognize him, wouldn't they? It would be a bit of a lark for them.

I'm sorry, she said to her guests, who were standing, too

casually, in the kitchen. I'd better press on with lunch for Sally. I have to see someone from the office this afternoon.

She stood in the doorway, framed by the dancing Tuscan pots in the wallpaper, with a crisp, apologetic smile. Of course, they bustled, we'll be out of here in a mo', let you get on. The house is looking marvellous, you know. Stunning.

Stunned, they left. At the end of the driveway, she heard a soft raucous growl that could have a been a motorbike. Or laughter.

Across the road, Evie's clock kept delicate time. Thin arms with heart-shaped tips grazed the ivory porcelain face. A bold gold fiddler in Louis XIV rig straddled the clock, the wire of his bow vibrating with each chime. On either side, gold metal flourishes tumbled down to the out-turned feet. Patsy found it hard to keep her eyes off the clock. She could imagine it in the grander house that Evie and Donald had owned before that difficult time with Donald's business.

Coffee here was served in porcelain cups, edged in gold. Evie's scarf was held at the neck with a cameo brooch bordered in gold filigree. She wore navy and white, sometimes a touch of red, occasionally in emergencies black, but black was so draining, except at night. Over the scarf she had draped a series of gold chains, antique. Her little fingers were weighted by solid settings of aquamarine and emerald, the pierced holes in her ears elongated by gold and pearl drops. Her thick shingled hair was the palest violet.

Patsy felt safe in Evie and Donald's house.

Evie was delighted to take Sally for an hour or so. She might like to take her little nap here on the sofa – what fun – or upstairs, it was all the same. Donald would be home in a minute but he adored Sally, Patsy knew that, and in any case he would be sleeping like a baby after lunch too.

"You are very fragile today, my darling Patsy," said Evie as a matter of fact. "It's a worry for you that Alan is away?"

"Not really," said Patsy, laughing. "It's easier in some ways – does that sound a dreadful thing to say? I just have to think about the children and everything runs like clockwork."

"Well, yes. It's true. One less to organize. But you miss him, also."

"Of course." She laughed again, as if apologizing. Evie remained silent. Patsy twisted around to watch Sally through the window transferring pebbles from the path to the perfect emerald lawn. "Oh Evie, I'm sorry. Let me put them . . ."

"Leave her. What's the harm? The little stones, we put them back later. It makes another game."

Evie hadn't shifted her gaze. Patsy twisted back, smiled briefly, took a sip of coffee and straightened the little silver spoon in the saucer.

She could no longer see them, but the bleached stones on the green were still painful to her. Sally was reckless and determined, capable of all kinds of outrage when Patsy wasn't there to modify her. Daytimes were a constant exercise in damage limitation. From the first, she had to prevent the children from arriving at school either late or insufficiently nourished or incorrectly dressed. When they got home, they burst open the order she'd so carefully tried to impose during the day. Sally always woke at the wrong moment or got into a cupboard or simply refused the routine that was so important to a child's security. And then when the routine was broken, Sally was upset. Of course. The mornings and evenings were terrible, shrill struggles. She could still hear herself, the edge of cruelty in her voice as she threatened and cajoled. In the evenings it was worse, like a nightmare variety act with spinning plates, one always about to fall. The children were forever finding one more task – I need a drink, I haven't finished my Geography colouring, my socks aren't clean for football, I'm still hungry, I don't want a bath, Mummy, I need to have some velvet and gold thread for Anne Boleyn's dress, where's blue teddy, Mummy? Mummy. I feel sick, I can't sleep, *why* can't we . . .?

How could she make any progress? She simply wasn't making any progress. And there was so much more to do.

When it was bad, and it was bad now – but that was only temporary, surely, in this unsettled period – she felt the rage descend in an instant. One moment she would be twirling at the centre of a maypole of demands, dispensing solutions, the next the whole structure had toppled and she was thrashing around, trying to cut a way out.

In the long run, it couldn't hurt them, the odd smack, although it would be so much better if she didn't have to do it. Jimmy just shrugged and skipped up the stairs, too proud to rub his arm. Lucy frightened her sometimes with her terrified look, the look that provoked Patsy to squeeze just a fraction harder, but Sally stared back, cool and judgemental, as if a three-year-old could judge. But they can't, can they?

Then the night would come and, eventually, the quiet of three children sleeping. She'd climb upstairs, voluntarily this time, and visit each one. The dark in their rooms was soothing and liberating. And they were so beautiful, the children, asleep. There was no one to see her stretch out alongside Jimmy in his ship's bunk, curving her body, despite the tight skirt, into an S behind his, stroking his hair back, feeling the slight wave of it beneath her palm. Kneeling beside Lucy, she traced the violet circles on the thin skin beneath her eyes, kissed the frown that nestled between the brows even in sleep, wanted to cry the tears for her. The hot plumpness of Sally in her little bed, the slightly acid smell of soap and infant sweat, made her salivate. Sometimes, she took the child's arm and kissed the soft white underside, gently taking a pinch of flesh loosely between her teeth, just to feel the weight and to bring the intoxicating smell closer to her nostrils. Or licked the hollow at the base of the throat, tempting fate. But if the heavy lashes should open then the two of them would be together like this, intimate, perfect . . .

Day and night.

"I'd better be getting back, Mr Rookin will be there at half past two." Evie nodded, bringing her gaze back from Sally in the garden. "I've no idea what all this is about, but it's connected with the head office in America, obviously. I get the impression it's good news; then again, I would expect to hear that from Alan. But the time difference of course, and he's working late and can't always get to a telephone . . ." Evie nodded again, but less definitely, inclining her head slightly.

"I do miss him, I suppose, Evie," Patsy said at last, and shrugged apologetically, "but there's so very little time to get everything done." She tugged at her hairband, anchoring it deeper in the lacquered gold. "Anyway, he doesn't miss us much. Far too busy, I'm sure. It must be very different over there – constant meetings, demands on his time and expertise."

"Are you perhaps a little angry with Alan, Patsy?"

Patsy sucked in her breath. "Oh Evie, is that the way it sounds? How dreadful. Of course not. Why should I be?"

"It's not impossible – sometimes I want to stab Donald with that little dagger, you know, the letter opener. You know?"

Patsy nodded, smiling. "You terrible woman. No, I'm not planning anything like that. Don't worry. There's no reason to be angry with Alan, except the usual. They forget; they're late; they're working too hard."

"Ah." Evie emptied the dregs from the cups into a little bowl. "Well, you had better get back."

"Yes," Patsy paused, relenting. "It's true, Evie. Sometimes, it feels as if Alan is, well, that we're in some kind of race. Against each other . . . Obviously, his work's important, but so is our home. Oh that does sound terrible . . . It does, doesn't it?"

"No. But I can't say I understand."

"Of course not, Evie. It's just me, I'm making no sense. Please take no notice. I really must go, thank you so much for the coffee, and for taking Sally. I'll come over as soon as Mr Rookin has gone. Sorry."

Patsy heard the slow tickle of Donald's key in the front door. She heard him negotiate the entrance, carefully putting down his briefcase to hang the key in a cupboard. Evie was already out of her seat, sleek and lively. She smoothed down her skirt and fairly skipped through the door. Patsy heard the kiss and the little hiatus of their embrace and the whisper.

"Oh, wonderful," Donald was saying as he came through the door, ducking a little from habit although the frame easily cleared his six and a quarter feet. "Darling," the address covered both Patsy and Sally who was grinning up at him shyly.

In his sixties, Donald had hit an eccentric elegance which had apparently evaded him in earlier decades, if photographs on the windowsills and piano were to be trusted. His height had been modified by an endearing stoop that gave his mournful face added comedy. The dark brows and crinkly hair streaked with white, not cosy silver, were less threatening. He was neither so thin nor apparently so serious. The long fingers and arms had grown theatrical, the better to illustrate the absurd stories he told against himself. He wore a family signet ring.

On some days, Donald could almost persuade Patsy that she could sing. Darling, I couldn't possibly play now, he'd protest, as he adjusted the stool backwards to accommodate his long legs and rifled through the curling books of old songs on the music rest. Out of the question. And he'd launch into "Just the Way You Look Tonight", or "Do Nothing Till You Hear From Me". At first Patsy just stood beside him, a little gauche. Donald would hum along, occasionally talking out particular phrases. Reveal how I feel about you. Some kiss may cloud my memory. Gradually, Patsy became a little bolder. I can't sing a note, she warned him. It would be ridiculous. Oh, but help me, he cajoled, just encourage me a little. And she tried a snatch or two, nothing obvious, the easy bit, the refrain. Donald would ease into the next song. Turn the page now, he'd call, and Patsy, pink from the effort, would lean forward and turn, with a little flourish. Excellent! he'd call. Come on, come on. Until one day, she found him supplying a harmony beneath her and broke off, giggling. Don't stop, he barked and she took up again.

At the end, he turned, took both her hands and kissed them. Oh. But. You're lovely. From the sofa, Evie applauded. Patsy felt she might cry.

Sometimes he and Evie were like newlyweds in their gloss paint and gilt love nest. She fussed over him, stroking that wild hair, smoothing out the creases in those long sleeves, giggling and teasing, professing exasperation. He affected not to understand her accent and looked down in bemusement at her pragmatic five-foot-nothing.

Sometimes, on weekends, Patsy heard their giggles across the close.

Fred Rookin was wearing a topcoat despite the sun. A light gabardine. He waited while Patsy hung it, and his hat, in the cupboard under the stairs – the only defence Alan had been able to marshal against open-tread.

The orange sofa resisted his presence. Rookin perched on the edge of the boxy upholstery. He stirred the sugar into the tea cup on the low table before him, touched the folder he'd already placed there, smiled and cleared his throat.

He was sure Alan would be telephoning her this evening and she could hear all the details. Things were, as he'd suspected they would, going well. Alan was doing them proud. A pause. She might have asked herself what would happen if his work did indeed deliver on its early promise. Had she asked herself that?

She supposed she had, but not seriously. After all, she knew so little. Fred Rookin followed the curve of her ankle.

Quite, well, that was the reason for his visit. The

prospect was now indeed that Alan would have to stay in America for rather longer than a few weeks.

How much longer might that be? Patsy tried to memorize the titles of the dozen or so books along the top of Alan's desk.

Hard to say, of course, but it might run to a year or so. Rookin observed the fascinating weave of her skirt.

A year? But he couldn't be away for that long, surely?

Well, obviously, he couldn't be apart from the family for that long. This was the question they had to address. And it was an exciting prospect for them all, some time in another country, in what, by all accounts was a beautiful area – opportunity, a tremendous adventure for the children, a prestigious assignment for Alan. They might consider themselves ambassadors for the Company.

And the house? For a moment, she was glad to have his full attention. What about the house?

Oh well, that need prove no problem. The Company could easily undertake to let the house for the period the family would be abroad. Carefully chosen tenants, of course. Essential items could be shipped, they would help with any necessary arrangements, just as, at the other end, there would be help with finding schools, accommodation and so on. She could see what he meant?

Patsy saw. It could all be arranged. She was being thrown from here, where it was hard enough to keep everything under control, to there where nothing was familiar, where everything was alien. But she wouldn't, she couldn't say that. There was nothing to say.

Fred Rookin, his duty discharged, eased back into the unyielding sofa, feeling behind him for support. He settled for the compromise of one foot off the floor in exchange for a relaxed yet masterful attitude.

Mrs Hopkins – may I call you Patsy? Thank you, Patsy – I know this is a little difficult to take in all at once, but you do seem to be taking the news very well, I must say. Very composed. And you must trust me. We will make this as easy as possible for you. We're all delighted for you, too.

Thank you.

You and I, he lifted one plump hand in an inclusive gesture, will have a great deal to organize in a relatively short time. I think we should aim to have you on the move as soon as the children's summer holidays begin. Give you a chance to settle in before the "vacation" ends over there, as it were.

I suppose that would be a good idea.

Rookin was sure that they could work together well. She was clearly a woman of impressive organization, looking around – which he did, briefly – it was obvious she could pull off wonders. Extraordinary. Distinctive. He scrutinized the tailoring on her blouse. She squeezed her knees together a little tighter and straightened her back. She looked down at the rug.

The rumble of the Humber on the loose gravel in the road announced the children's return. Patsy stood up, relieved, and went to the door. James and Lucy trooped in. The driver, Jon (or was it Jonny?), remained a few steps behind, out on the lawn.

"Please," she said to him, "Come in. There's a cup of tea. Thank you for collecting the children."

He looked surprised. "Are you sure? I can wait in the car. It's no problem."

"No, of course. But please do. Please." She gestured him in.

Fred Rookin nodded at the younger man, who stood awkwardly in the living room doorway. Patsy motioned to him to sit down.

"I have just been discussing with Mrs Hopkins, Jon, the fact that her husband's work will take the entire family to America for a year or so. Which is very exciting. Isn't it, Patsy? . . . Mrs Hopkins." He twitched a little.

The children swung round to their mother. "Look, darlings, I'll tell you all about it properly in a moment." Her voice was high, nasal with strain. "Nothing's happening today or tomorrow – it will all take time, so you mustn't worry. I'll tell you everything later. Well, what I know, anyway."

"Children," intoned Rookin, as they sat mutely beside him on the sofa, munching Battenburg. "You will have to help your mother over the next few weeks. As I will be doing." Patsy found an object of interest out through the window. "And indeed, Jon will be doing, helping you to pack away those toys you might need in the US of A. So you'll have to make lists, you know."

The children looked at Jon, Jimmy spreading ink-stained hands in a gesture of incredulous triumph, Lucy frowning from beneath her brows. Jon grinned reassurance back.

"Inventories, Jon. The rental people will need those. Shippers, travel arrangements, we've got to get all this moving as soon as possible. I'll give you an outline when we get back to the office." Rookin manoeuvred himself off the sofa.

In the hall, Patsy fetched his coat and hat from under the stairs. "Thank you, Mrs Hopkins," he articulated, seeking out her eyes. She coloured slightly and adjusted the belt on her skirt, turning away.

"Did you . . .?" She appealed to Jon. "No, of course you didn't. No coat." He shook his head.

"Isn't that a striking colour, Jon, that Mrs Hopkins is wearing today? As always, of course. I must say, Mrs Hopkins, you do have the most extensive wardrobe."

Jon cleared his throat. "I expect she needs it, sir. To put all those clothes in."

Rookin glanced sharply across at his assistant. For an instant Patsy's shoulders relaxed, but she kept her eyes on the parquet.

6

*D*EAR JIMMY, *Lucy and Sal,*
        Out of my window I can see cars as wide as the living room, skyscrapers as tall as that hot-air balloon we saw at the fête last summer (well over five hundred feet, Jimmy, rather dwarf that Post Office tower we're planning, I'm afraid) and my bedroom is the size of the village hall. At least.

I haven't got the knack of the hours here yet. I still keep waking up at half past four or five o'clock. No bad thing because everyone seems to start work at half past seven or eight sharp. All in their brightly coloured cars — red stripes and fins, Jimmy. Here's a drawing.

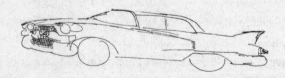

And girls, sometimes people eat breakfast in their cars. They take it away from roadside cafés in special boxes, with plastic knives and forks and cups that keep the drinks warm. Each in a little compartment of its own. Like this.

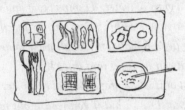

I think of you lot then, all round the table in the kitchen, fried bread and eggs, sausage and bacon on Saturday. When you get here I'll show you the menus in some of these places. They reach down to your knees!

I hope you're all helping Mummy prepare for the move. She's bound to be a bit sad, isn't she, leaving her lovely house that she's made so special for us? But, I'll tell you what, the house here will be really exciting. You can each have your own room – and most of these places come with a big playroom. The Americans are very good at playing. Some of the grown-ups even have playrooms too – with big trophies on the wall, elk or even bear. Perhaps we'll all go hunting one day, Davy Crockett hats on, marching in line, height order. And there'll be a television of course and a big garden. I even went to someone's house the other day and they had a swimming pool right outside their kitchen door! Sausage, bacon – and splash in the water!! Well perhaps not splash straight away, we know about that one-hour rule.

Have to go now. Back to the plant, you'll be able to go on a trip around it on one of the open days, Jimmy. You too perhaps, *girls. But not my laboratory, I'm afraid. Too secret.*

Actually, there's no great mystery — just a mixture of carbon, like coal or charcoal, oxygen, which (remember?) we breathe all around us in the air, and hydrogen which is part of water. So there it is, half a glass of water, a lump of coal and a hiccup. Well, more or less, anyhow. Whizz 'em all up together — wheeeee! Sooner or later (let's hope sooner, shall we?) some new substance will emerge that can be spun into thread.

And the best of it is the proper official chemistry name. I won't give it to you exactly . . . but if you read it out really fast — and you didn't bother with all the little numbers dotted here and there — it would sound rather like this . . . chooooo . . . choooo . . . coooooooohoooohoooooh . . . like a little dove.

So long, chickens,

Daddy

(In the eleven years that they've known each other, Patsy has only once received a letter from Alan, a few days before her first visit to his family. It contained a joke about a fellow student and a list of things to bring on the train. His writing is hard to read, tiny and cramped, although the ys, js and fs are curiously looped, almost girlish. Occasionally, he leaves her notes ("mark on shirt!!" "green tie?") which though terse, are not offensive, since he leaves them in surprising places like the kitchen windowsill or the back of the bathroom door. He's obviously made some calculation as to the best moment to catch her attention. With the children, however, he can be more fulsome. At Christmas, since he has little prior knowledge of the presents that he and Patsy give the children, he writes them long and slightly fanciful messages in their cards, which the girls are too excited to read or have read to them although Jimmy frowns and tucks his away upstairs in his atlas, for later. Patsy has no such archive – but why would she need one? Alan's hardly the love-letter type; it would be almost embarrassing, wouldn't it? All the same, she is surprised by the letter and wonders, just for a moment, what he might one day write to her, if the mood ever took him.)

Ray's wife Marian places a tanned hand on Alan's arm to warn him of the step. It's not that he can't see it; it's just that it may be deeper than he's expecting. People, she adds, looking sideways under heavily defined lids, are always losing their footing. If she doesn't take the precaution of warning them.

Alan is grateful. He watches his step. Marian's matador jacket is emerald green, silk, he thinks, like the bandeau that flattens her dark curls. Ava Gardner, Alan? I haven't heard much about *her* in a while. But I'm flattered, anyway. Thank you. She smiles and turns her head slightly, so he observes the kittenish tilt of her nose.

They are perched at diagonals across the "conversation pool", a sunken pit that squares up to Ray and Marian's baronial hearth. On three sides great slabs of stone have been hewn into tiers. Deep cushions turn them into seats. As he perches, Alan's hands are resting either side of his thighs in the stringy fleece of some beast.

He turns at the sound of Ray's footsteps and expert whistling, but at this level all he can see are fine camel socks and loafers. Ray makes a neat entrance down the steps, balancing three highballs and humming, clinking the ice in the glasses in rhythm to the melody.

Ray and Marian have been hospitality itself. They have extended their open-plan home to him. Weekends are a big feature of Ray and Marian's life. That's when they throw open the doors, turn up the hi-fi and party. Their children have entered, or hover on the threshold of, the sherbet tunnel of dating, so what alternative do they have? Become the forbidding monsters their parents were – or create a home where the kids will want to bring their friends? In any case, there's plenty of room for the two generations to coexist – and to be frank, Alan, they'd rather the kids were fooling about in the playroom than in the back of the car. As Ray always maintains, if you're big enough – you're old enough. In Delaware, it isn't only the tax laws that are more relaxed.

Alan nods admiringly, calculating the distance in yards from the glass-fronted living area to the subterranean teenage den with its windows out on to the pool deck. Even with Ray's deft footwork it would take minutes to negotiate those deep stages out of the stone pit, the straits of long polished hardwood floor, the islands of pale rug, the treacherous promontories of low tables, not to mention the detours around sheer cliffs of glass enclosure where cactus, fig and full-sized trees all flourish. Inside the house. Alan wonders at the teenage transgressions that could be accomplished in those minutes.

If an Englishman's home is his castle, then what term can Alan find to describe this rambling fort of Ray and Marian's? Their house is draped across landscaped hillocks which resemble a small golf course. Its great windows gaze down past the curve of drive to a private road below. Its garage door rolls heavenwards to welcome Ray's broad slice of car. A plume of pampas grass waves like a standard by the giant pebbles that lead to the front door.

It is, Alan can see, a good place to spend time. Ray presides over the bar and leads sparring sessions with the punch bag in the den. He divides groups into teams for games in the pool. He'll be there at the barbecue, supervising, tweaking, turning the steaks just before they char. Not "cooking", of course. He is fast and funny. To most of the people, most of the time.

Above all, Ray is a consummate planner. He can give Alan the impression that his considerable energies are largely deployed in the arrangement of weekends, evenings and holidays. On this side of the Atlantic, Alan finds, the spare time, do-it-yourself, bookends of time off from work are transformed into broad vistas of opportunity. Florida, the Lakes, Coronado or St Croix – place-names are bandied about between his new colleagues as targets that rank with sales, turnover and market penetration.

This is a development he can respect, but not yet

understand. Ray is even now holding the floor (does he have another stance?) with an exposition of next weekend's tennis tournament. He's concerned about the timing of the mixed doubles. Does it allow for cocktails at six-thirty? Anyway, that little contest can be despatched in a half-hour or so; the real business on the court will have been over between the men earlier in the afternoon. Marian smiles at Alan from beneath the black slick on her lids. Alan smiles back, shyly. Ray claps him on the back and joins in.

Ray applies the same efficiency to work. He wants to look after Alan so that Alan can deliver for the firm – and for himself, of course. This division of the corporation is very exciting – has been for fifteen years or so, thanks to Dr Carothers and nylon. You people did wonderful stuff with Terylene, but with Dacron – well, you have to admit, Alan, we had the edge. And frankly, the ball is in our court now. We're the only ones who have the muscle to deploy these new polyesters.

In Bettesville Alan is struck by the old-money feel of the corporation. He hadn't expected the caramelized portraits in the halls. His colleagues point out the creamy green and gold oil studies of grand houses with jutting fountains; they're museums and country clubs now, he'll have to take the kids and Patsy to visit on weekends. Then there's the university and the children's hospital and the art gallery – and this is just in one town. The corporation is expanding at an impressive rate.

One evening, Ray hauls him away from the laboratory bench and they drive down the valley to a lake. Artificial, Alan calculates, but the water stretches away in front of him like a roll of platinum leaf and it's a relief from the modulated woods that alternate with the avenues and circuses of Bettesville. They eat in a timber glassed-in restaurant suspended on piers over the water. Ray points out to Alan a long shed in the distance, just at the point where the lake feeds back into the river.

"See that, Alan? The brown roof with the out-buildings? Looks small from here, I suppose. Well, it *is* small, I guess. When I was a kid that was a sawmill, fell into disuse round the time I stopped coming down to fish here. No demand. Bigger mechanized mills upriver. Until this year. Know what's starting up there? New mill, but textiles this time. Might not seem worth it when the big guys are just down the road turning out square miles of the stuff. But that's the joy of what we're doing – new modifications, new fabrics and new possibilities for small firms to operate. Under licence, of course.

"You know," and, as Ray finishes chewing a piece of crawfish, he bounces the edge of an emphatic palm lightly on Alan's arm, "they're even taking over old gas stations and selling polyester garments direct to the public. Don't you just love how the world turns around? The miracle of oil – wondrous stuff, stuff of our lives. It's like those illustrations they make you do as a kid – all the uses from this one drop."

Alan nods, laughs. Sitting in class, at the desk by the brown-painted hot-water pipes, he'd been transfixed by a poster of a scientist in a white coat, who held up a test tube of a coppery substance, squinting authoritatively at it, while turning a resolute jaw towards the equally coppery sunlight breaking through the window.

"No, seriously, Alan," Ray's smile broadens. "Seriously." Alan is mesmerized by his teeth, which are not as even and white as they one day will be, but pretty damn impressive even so. "This kind of arrangement could be very beneficial to your own country. Help with the rebuilding." As Alan makes to interrupt, he corrects himself. "That's not to say that you haven't made a magnificent job in Britain. My God, we of all companies appreciate that. Magnificent. Truly magnificent."

Alan smiles back, magnificent himself in the late evening sun. He appreciates Ray's intentions and his national generosity. There is something very appealing about being the promising newcomer, the late starter, the Benjamin. Alan is proving to Ray that decadence and war have not deadened the British spirit and Ray in turn is rewarding him with manly consideration and encouragement. This is not friendship as Alan has known it before; this is more like courtship – and it feels, for now, with that hum of mutual advantage and understanding, twenty-four carat.

In the neon dawn of the laboratory, Alan takes what he

and his three assistants recognize for differing reasons as a superior approach. In part, his nervousness makes him less flexible; more British, they reckon. He makes firm and decisive statements a little too often; he walks up and down just a fraction more than is strictly practical; he has not yet discovered the Dictaphone in any useful way.

Following at a respectful distance, Petersen, Strachan and di Stefano are frustrated by this courtesy that also dictates. Would they be so good as to? Could they see their way to? They are amused, then irritated by apologies that preface a kind of rudeness, in their opinion. He is sorry, but could they begin that process again, with a lower precipitation threshold? Life is circumscribed with irritations. This is tedious, that is dreadfully inconvenient – *but* . . . After a couple of days of exasperation – can't the man say what he wants plain and simple? – they find they are treading cautiously lest they stumble against the wrong side of that *but*.

Alan has no time to look up because, in the pursuit of his grail, he is wrestling with phantoms. In the synthetics field, openness is a veil for absolute secrecy. Rival organizations share information about achievements in a flutter of fine paper pamphlets at conferences. These butterflies settle in time into articles in professional journals. Everything is noted, yet nothing revealed. The method and significance of each new fibre that springs off the scientist's bench may be detailed in public but for commercial reasons its constitution remains secret until the licence expires. A frieze of sprightly characters from

Arnel to Orlon parades through Alan's head, vivid but flat, lacking the dimension of empirical proof.

Alan is sure he's on to something exciting, but can't be sure no one else isn't. He has just one week for testing.

Petersen and di Stefano haul in the grey-green enamelled machine while Strachan lines up the squared paper and balances the pencil in its cradle. A length of the fibre is already there on the bench in a tight glistening skein. The first hurdle was to spin from the solid – it held the required density, but it's early days yet. Nothing in Strachan, or Petersen or di Stefano's expression indicates any expectation of this next trial. They are obedient to a fault.

From a spool on the machine with its dials and calibrations Petersen threads the fibre, milky-white, guiding it one, two, three and a half feet along the bench at shoulder height. Slowly, he lowers it towards the receiving apparatus, fastening it carefully on to the bobbin, twisting clockwise with the flex. Behind him, di Stefano makes a minute adjustment to the metal eye on the top of the master machine, and gently depresses a switch that sends a beam of yellow light to the corresponding aperture on the smaller device, confirming the truth of the alignment. Strachan straightens the pencil as it hovers over the graph paper.

This morning they are beginning a twelve-hour test for stress-strain.

With a click, the lumpen machine begins to pull on the pearly string. The tiniest tremor passes along the line. Alan watches the first contraction; sometimes this opening tug, however gentle, can be catastrophic. It's a particular characteristic of this group of compounds that, if one thread breaks, the individual filaments splay out. There are numerous advantages to a synthetic yarn of this type, if it works, but no second chance, no evolutionary backstop that sheep or cotton-bush affords. Alan turns away, he can't exhaust himself with excessive concern at this stage; there are hours ahead.

It could be worse, in any case. Fibres with the softest handle don't respond well to twelve hours on the rack but softness and, to a degree, drape are not a priority in this case. Or so Ray tells him. What he is led to believe *is* important is that the fibre should not hold excess water. Ambient moisture has dragged down the performance of too many of this yarn's predecessors. So for two days Alan's baby has lain in a tepid bath, stirred only by the spatula in di Stefano's thin concerned hand. This morning, the data were encouraging. Although sodden, the fibre began to feel dry to the touch when only eighty-one per cent of the moisture had been mangled from it. Eighty-one per cent – a congruence of basins, measuring vases, notebooks and di Stefano's dry, shiny finger poking gently at the tangled nest of fibre.

This is the one, thinks Alan. Has to be.

Ray drops by around eleven. He looks over shoulders, nods appreciatively and winks at Alan. Alan doesn't respond; the contractions are coming more frequently now. Looking good, Alan. If it carries on like this, we'd like to see you around what – three-thirty? That would have given it seven and a half hours, right? Now, we'll assume adequate elasticity and so on. The boys here can verify that later. I want you to assemble all the ratios, notes on performance et cetera and we'll meet in the conference suite, level five.

Carry on it does and, on the stroke of half past three, Alan presents himself before the relevant technical directors, having left a telephone extension number with the lab, in case of emergency.

The room is large, but he's ceased to wonder at the acres of hardwood. He expects long glossy tables to be arranged in quadrilaterals of one form or another, making him wonder on one occasion if he shouldn't duck underneath and perform a little song and dance routine in the middle. Mostly, he doesn't have time for frivolous thoughts. He's never had to concentrate quite this hard for quite this long, which in its way is exciting.

Alan isn't nervous now; his preoccupation with the pearly thread three storeys down precludes nerves. Later, he will marvel at his detachment when confronted with the men who conceived of the fabrics that clothed America. For their part, the greying half-dozen are tetchy with post-prandial acid and anticipated disappointment. It's another trial, another blind alley; nothing has ever come close to that first big discovery more than twenty years earlier – it's their misfortune to have been born in the lifetime of the man who invented nylon.

They quiz him gruffly. They sniff disapproval and haul at the crescent waistbands of their trousers, easing themselves on the tight upholstered leather seats. They want to know specificity and density. Has he attempted dye absorption? Well, maybe it *is* too early; it'll probably not come to that, in their experience. Dye is, in any case, a subject that makes them reach for the Pepto-Bismol. They all remember the volatile dyes, with the real small molecules, how they plain floated away when shoulders and pockets were heat-pressed, the way the British liked to? How that Lovat green, kind of a subtle moss colour, gave way to patches of bright emerald? They shudder and guffaw at the memory. Don't want anything like that here, do we?

Alan does not allow himself to deal in probabilities. He limits himself strictly to the data certified so far, and that flow of ratio and measurement pours over them like milk of magnesia. His tone is eager but deferential. He offers his findings but bows to the obelisk of their wisdom. Ray, sitting a little to one side and behind them, nods encouragement.

Maybe, Ray interjects at a suitable interval, with a little announcing cough, it would be useful – if they thought it appropriate – to outline the use to which the fibre might be applied.

Oh well, conclude the elders churlishly, as if the business were at an end. If you feel it's timely or even necessary . . . over to you, then, and they turn towards a slightly younger man with serious glasses. He rises and advances to the lectern. Alan hangs back, at a loss, one hand on the frame of his flip chart, no place to sit.

"Gentlemen," begins the man, and Ray obligingly brings forward a shrouded board, which he unveils to reveal an image of a young woman in a bright yellow dress trimmed with white. Her pillbox hat peeps over the crown of her head which is tilted back with laughter, or admiration. She is sitting on a low wall, flanked by two immaculate young men. "We are on the verge of the most exciting development since the loom. We are poised to build on the success of the Gunnessi-Cale findings." The young men's attention is on her and her reaction to their entertaining company. But the attention of the audience is on them, and more precisely, on the grey and charcoal jackets and trousers they sport, barely creasing as they bend their arms to flex a cigarette or point to some diversion out of frame. "If we can indeed perfect a fabric that looks and feels like a wool mixture, but with little of the moisture retention, then we are truly close to the goal of the wash'n'wear suit."

Three floors down, Alan hears the squeal of fibres stretched to exhaustion. On the spindle a filament bumps over its brothers, yanked unequally by the inexorable tug of the bulky testing machine. The little filament begins to twist, sending warning pulsations through the bunch.

7

IF PAUL NEWMAN hadn't appeared that week at the Odeon, hustling, the eyes of Mr Rookin's assistant Jon might not have attracted comment from Mandy Martin as she helped Patsy clear one-legged toys and piles of scribbled paper out of the children's cupboard. Sally toddled about in a nest of dressing-up remnants.

"Fascinating colour, of course, Patsy. Blue, but pale blue, almost aquamarine. And dark lashes – you wouldn't believe it if he was a woman."

"No?" said Patsy, raising a sable brow.

They hacked at the punctured tambourines and pieces of string. Newman had been in between them all day, levelling those startling eyes at each in turn, resting his chin on his hand by the windowsill, angling denimed hips. He added tension to an atmosphere already charged with clearing out. Shoes discarded, their feet padded between cool tiles and woollen rug, sorting the candidates for jumble sale or dustbin – paintboxes with muddy squares of caked pigment, skipping ropes with one loose handle or a teddy bear with a wisp of escaped stuffing. An intermediate pile appeared – might come in useful. The pile grew larger. They won't miss these, you know, said Mandy, after twenty minutes or so. Anyway, there'll be new toys, better toys, bigger ones. You won't need all this stuff. Patsy stared at the hillock of childhood.

Mandy sliced into her gaze with a thumb-size tree fashioned from a remnant of soap, a lolly stick and painted wire wool. "Will Jimmy insist on the train set, then?"

Patsy sank down to the rug. What would it seem like there, the little oval of locomotives drawing wagons of matchsticks and sugar crystals? Bryant & May, Tate & Lyle, chugga-chugga-chug, the crazed bridge and the clothes-peg signalman, mirror pond and cottonwool sheep, crushed by the packing, emerging at the other end sluggish and shabby.

"Storage," she sighed. "Can't compete with those Pullman coaches, or shiny Chevrolets. All that chrome. Or space rockets – what's the point?"

"Good," Mandy was stern. Even if the initiative couldn't be hers, she'd taken on the executive role in the exercise. They turned again to the cupboard, sniffing a little from the cocktail of dust and old glue.

Patsy was picking up speed. Free of the children's clutter, this little room on the side of the kitchen, cosy with the water pipes, could be a snug, a television room even. She began to see the house as potential tenants might. Professional people from abroad, perhaps, with a continental eye for the open-plan.

They worked fast, exchanging observations, a little more brittle as they progressed. No getting away from it, while Mandy was staying behind Patsy was entering a league beyond A New Summer Brightness for the Bathroom. But there was a race still between them, a studied comparison, while each claimed to be An Absolute Disaster, All Over the Place. Would you believe it?

Patsy's days hung on the framework of Alan's telephone calls. The day before, the day of, the day after. Once she heard his voice, Patsy felt she must exude capability, challenging his. It would have to be some miraculous fibre he'd discovered to compete with the speed and strength of her arrangements. He was typically imprecise on the practicalities of the move, preferring in their brief conversations to enthuse generally – on the space, the speed, the opportunity – and that enthusiasm seemed so impractical, so childish, that she couldn't absorb it. When Alan's letter arrived for the children, she listened tolerantly as Jimmy read it aloud with spiralling glee. When Alan spoke to her, on the other hand, his sympathy for the task of packing up the house was controlled, as if he really didn't wish to be drawn into all that.

"He's not so tall, when you see him standing up, though, is he?" Mandy continued.

"Paul Newman?"

"Well him too, it's true. I meant Jon, Jonny, whatever his name is. Actually."

Patsy considered. "I suppose not. About average? I've usually only seen him behind the wheel."

"And his fiancée . . ." A heavy pause.

Patsy looked up. "What about her? I don't think I even knew he was engaged."

"She's the head-waitress at the Tudor Rose. You know, the dark one?"

Patsy searched, shook her head.

"Well," Mandy paused.

"Sounds ominous," Patsy folded a small nurse's apron around a rubber stethoscope.

"She's not exactly what you'd expect."

"And what am I expecting?"

"He's a good-looking boy, you have to admit."

Patsy looked out through the leaded panes. It was still raining. "Yes. I suppose. Charming more than handsome, though."

"Well, she's neither."

Patsy laughed. "Oh dear, poor Jonny."

"And she's definitely older. Into her thirties, I should think. It's very strange."

"A mystery, Mandy. I'll expect bulletins in Bettesville."

"Oh, I'm sure." Their eyes met. Patsy smiled, briefly, and returned to the pile in front of her, concentrating on the folding, uncomfortable.

"You must have had enough of this by now," she said and gathered up the remainders. "Is it really that late? You shouldn't be bothering with all this old nonsense."

"Heavens," said Mandy, taking the cooler cue, twisting

to look at the clock, "you're right – I must dash. Almost time to collect Timmy from nursery." She spelt it out, formally, as if their very corpuscles were not ruled by the tidal movements of the daily schedule. "Sally darling," she said, turning to the child, "will you come and play with Timmy soon, give Mummy some time to get everything packed?"

Perhaps when they got back she could achieve something more dramatic in the bedroom. The deep pink, with that black rug – she still yearned for a black carpet but the effect of the rug was much the same – would be all over by then. Finished. Come to think of it, the Venetian masks, crossed over the bedhead, were perhaps a touch unnecessary, even vulgar. Too southern European, perhaps: influences were shifting north. Alan wouldn't mind: the whole place would need redecorating after the tenants anyway, that was all built into the rental agreement. And the new fireplace downstairs would be an investment, a striking one. The house needed drama, a big gesture.

Ideas ran around like mercury. Nothing persisted in her mind for more than a few minutes. Sentences scurried out, never quite reaching a full stop. The children, their clothes, their toys, their rooms, tidying of, storage versus shipping, informing friends and distant family of the move, schools, doctors and dentists . . . arranging a foster family for the cat (why had she relented on a cat? There were hairs everywhere. It wasn't even sleek and neat like Holly Golightly's Cat. *That* never coughed furballs on to the doormat.), having the carpets and curtains steam-cleaned, meeting with the lawyers and the mortgage company to arrange power of attorney and continued payments. Cancelling her life for twelve months or more. Preparing to go unprepared into strangeness.

She walked three paces into a room and couldn't recall why she was there. She wrote lists and left them in alcoves or by the second step of the stairs. At night she woke, her heart galloping to some vital task overlooked, but by the morning she'd forgotten what it was and replaced it on the first list of the day with other important, but substitute tasks. The nights were endless, the days marathons. She could finish nothing, interrupted by the children, or the telephone or the crackles in her brain, despatching her down another trail.

On the stairs, the vacuum cleaner toppled down a couple of steps, splitting open yet again to disgorge a wedge of mouse-coloured fluff. Alan had despised its spherical design from the beginning. It's just a gimmick, he'd said, still the same old mechanism, but under a space-agey round lid. She'd loved it, though; it reminded her of a little robot dog trotting through the house, snuffling up the dirt, cat hairs mainly, of course. It was surprisingly cumbersome: you had to really tug it and then, suddenly, it would lurch off in the most unpredictable way.

When she got there, it would be different. There'd

probably be another system entirely. Fresh start, blank canvas. Alan was right. There was no point in looking back.

The first tear was a surprise. Decades later, with a therapist, she will construct a rational pyramid of demands and constraints which lead to this soggy apex. It will always worry her that she couldn't explain why the tears should have come then, in front of a small man who smelt of sawdust, singed wire and stale tobacco.

The local builder was perplexed by this latest request – a fireplace with a fireproof window. Heat, but behind glass, and all set square and modern. She'd have to be very clear, so he didn't get it wrong. He wasn't sure he could altogether see the point of it. She'd have to be on hand for consultation, *if* she wasn't too busy. He replaced the little notebook in the breast pocket of his putty-tinted overalls and squinted up at her. He smiled his challenge; the gold clips on his dentures winked.

"It's quite clear," she said, turning to the wall and sweeping her hand across the white brickwork. "The flue is *here*, so you have to put the connecting er, column, *there*, I want the hearth *here*, with the draught mechanism and so on. Sliding glass door, like on a cabinet but with fireproof glass."

"Hold on a minute now, Mrs Hopkins," said the builder, laughing softly as though she'd made an indecent proposal. "Steady, steady." He turned slightly for support to his assistant, whose purple ears sprouted silver tufts. "I don't want to be difficult, but there are regulations. And there are tests we have to do."

"But it was a working fireplace. Just a year ago. You blocked it up. You must remember."

"Oh, we remember. But what you're proposing isn't a simple question of putting back. Is it? We're not trying to be difficult." His assistant shook his head, vigorously. "We just need more specific instructions." He paused, scrutinizing the skirting board, then lifted his glance suddenly, enlightened, as if a shaft of sunlight had hit the offending wall. "Ah. Do you have any drawings, Mrs Hopkins? Because if, by chance, you had drawings . . .?" The assistant nodded, encouragingly.

"If that's what you need, I'll make sure you have them," said Patsy tartly and at that point the traitor slid down from the corner of her right eye. She caught it with the back of her hand before it reached the cheekbone, drawing in breath and turning away in an instant. "Excuse me, I need to get something from the kitchen," she exhaled and hurried out.

In the overcast light, the diagonals on the tiled floor were jagged. She swallowed, pushing down the sob, and ran a glass of water from the tap. By her hip, the twin-tub whirred reassuringly, delivering spurts of milky water into the sink from its drainage hose. The bulk of the fridge reproached her for weakness, for wasting time and energy when there were so many other things to be done. But the fireplace had become a priority. The priority. If she could only get that right, she wouldn't be ashamed to leave the house.

The door bell rang. The two builders in the living room fell silent. Smoothing down her dress, running her fingertips under her eyes to check for swelling, Patsy walked steadily to the front door. She recognized Jonny's outline, the waves in his hair exaggerated by the dimples in the glass.

"Hello. Do come in, but it's not the most convenient moment. The builders are here."

"Oh, I see," he said. "Would you like me to come back another time? It's only that Mr Rookin has sent these forms for you to sign. And there's a schedule, a travel schedule," he couldn't hide a certain self-consciousness at the importance of the phrase, "for you to see – and approve, of course. It has to be . . ." he steeled himself, "confirmed in the next couple of days – but there's no hurry now." He seemed caught between efficiency and curiosity.

"No, please. Just as well now as any time." As he scrutinized her face, she willed the redness to subside.

"It won't take a moment. Where would you like me to put them?"

From the stairs above, they heard Sally's waking cry. Patsy sighed. Her hand rose halfway to her head, "Oh dear." She stood, rooted, staring at the papers in Jonny's hand.

"Perhaps I can help," he said. "Do you need to speak to the builders?"

She nodded, and then shook her head, angrily. "Well, I haven't . . . It's so stupid. Oh, I can't seem to make them understand." She trailed off, peevish.

"Shall we go into the kitchen for a moment?" Jonny looked up at the landing again. They listened. "Seems to have gone quiet." He grinned at Patsy. "Shall we?"

She nodded, pushing a strand of hair back into place. In the kitchen, he shut the door and put the papers on the table. "We can deal with those in a minute. Now, what about the builders?"

She explained about the fireplace, its location and importance in the scheme of the room. He listened seriously. "Do you think it's ridiculous?" The question was superfluous: he couldn't possibly answer it. Of course it was ridiculous, but she did want it.

He didn't react. "I've never heard of anything like it, but then I wouldn't have, would I? Doesn't sound impossible, though. And they say they want drawings? Do you have any?"

"Well, no, of course not."

"Have you got a piece of paper?"

"Yes, why?"

Under her supervision, he sketched a rough diagram. He used to be apprenticed to an electrician, he said, always drafting wiring plans. Anyway, the builders knew what to do, really, they were just testing her. She smiled, at last. It's all to do with confidence, he said, it's all a bit of a con. You give them this, and tell them your husband drew it up. I'm sorry, but that's how it is.

"Heavens, you don't have to apologize. Thank you, anyway." The wobble had darted back into her voice. She turned back to the side and took a gulp of water. He looked down. "I'll do it now," she said.

He was looking at her again now, curiously. "Look, give yourself a minute. They can wait. Or would you like me to do it?"

"No," she was shocked. "No, no. I'll do it now." She hesitated.

"You look very calm," he said, "composed. Like you always do. 'Mrs Hopkins'," he added, with a neat imitation of Rookin's caress. "I'll hang on with these papers for when you've finished."

It was Evie who had antennae for this kind of thing. That boy, she'd said as she and Patsy were sorting the garden tools into categories suitable for inventory, that boy likes women. It's wonderful, don't you think?

"Oh, I don't think he's particularly fast, Evie," protested Patsy, not sure what she meant herself.

"Fast, fast," muttered Evie, impatiently. "You talk nonsense sometimes, if you don't mind me saying. Steady and disinterested, that's better?"

"Does Donald like women, Evie?" Patsy asked and was immediately horrified at the presumed intimacy. "I mean, to talk to, spend time with?"

"Yes, darling. He does. But while he does that, other people steal his money. Sometimes it's not such a good arrangement." She peered out beneath the violet fringe.

They laughed. Patsy thought of the red and cream leather albums of photographs in Evie and Donald's house, and of Donald squinting lazily through a curl of cigarette smoke at his wife behind the camera, caught in the morning sun on a Riviera balcony, the silver pots and broken rolls and crumpled napkins of a leisurely breakfast lying abandoned on the little table before him.

Years later, when she remembered that afternoon in the kitchen, which she often did, the conversation was fuller, somehow. He surely made observations about things she did, the way she looked, that revealed his concern, the attention he'd paid to her every movement. Without doubt, he thought those things, even if he didn't actually speak the words. How could he have done? Men didn't in those days: they hadn't learnt yet.

Recalled later, their conversation over the tenancy agreement lasted more than an hour. Well over half an hour, at least. You can say a great deal in that time. What could he do to make it all simpler for her? What did she want? Each section took a minute or two longer than it might have done. But not long enough.

At last all the boxes on the sheets were ticked and signed. Sally was downstairs with them now and Jonny had pushed her around the kitchen floor in a packing case balanced on her little trolley. Patsy laughed along with the child's shrieks of excitement. She remembered that, the concentration on his face as he manoeuvred between the chairs. When he looked up, triumphant at a racing turn, it was a glance cleared of diffidence or reserve or resentment or any other accessories either of them might have put in there. She can still summon up the pleasure of that look.

Then she dropped the jug. That heavy cut-glass pitcher, a wedding gift. What was she doing, clambering up on the side, reaching up across that cardboard box? No, no – I'm fine, thank you, she'd protested, her back to him. Don't worry, I know where everything is. Busy, busy. She'd had the heavy base of it, right there in her hand when something gave way. Perhaps it was her knees rolling over on the Formica, or her wrist, or a sudden giddiness, whatever the cause one moment there was a weight, the next a crash. Chunks of glass spun across the floor.

Careful, he said, scooping Sally up from the trolley. I'll give you a hand down. Don't cut yourself.

No, I'm fine, she said, crossly. So stupid. She picked her way across the ice floes of glass. Take Sally round the corner into the playroom, would you? Just make sure she stays out of the way. She can hear her tone even now, accusing almost, as if he has been compliant in that moment of light-headedness that ended in shards. From the cupboard under the stairs she retrieved the dustpan and brush and an old cushion to kneel on as she swept furiously into the corners, hiding her blushes, shovelling the glass into the dustpan. Her face was hot, she felt her dress squeezing against her hips. She mustn't get up in a hurry – well, she might keel over for a start – but she wasn't sure the seams could take the strain. What a fool.

In the playroom the laughter had subsided. Sally was singing gently to herself but the infectious euphoria of the game had gone. Patsy reached around behind her for a cloth, curving her body, one hip jutting out. Her eyes fell on the cloth and then beyond, to his feet in the playroom doorway. She looked up to his face. His expression was watchful and intense; it frightened her a little, made her catch her breath. He caught her glance, and quickly turned away.

When arranging a room, it is still (for all the freedom of modern design) advisable to have a focal point. Then you may like to offset your main feature, a fireplace or a picture window or some interesting example of modern art with a couple of significant objects: a pair of armchairs, for example, or an armchair and a sofa. Be aware, as you place them, of the effect they may have on one another. Ask yourself these key questions.

When was the moment that she first began to anticipate his visits, to feel for the displacement of air when he stood in a doorway?

Whenever it was, it was the moment that would crystallize the world, make it clear and vivid, like the opening shot of a movie. It was the moment that would make life perfect, and spoil it for ever.

There was nothing and everything remarkable about him. He was a pleasant enough looking young man, as her mother might say, with complex eyes. Like Paul Newman, of course. But in which role?

He seemed considerate, beyond what he'd been asked to do. He might be quiet, but by no means slow. When he'd first accompanied the rental agent, he'd asked a few questions, intelligent enquiries that might not have occurred to her. Or was she keeping quiet, hoping he would step into a kind of intimacy, that suggested to this third party, this letting expert, that they enjoyed some greater trust than they did? That he was her stand-in husband in some unspoken game?

What had happened the first time he had smiled at her? Not turned up the corners of his mouth while he held open a car door for her, but conveyed some pleasure in her very existence, in the simple fact of being near her or hearing her speak – an audacious pleasure that shot through to her, bowling down her veins. Why did he risk this?

Perhaps he was being nice. Perhaps she was so good at manners that she could bully other people into them, too.

Why did he move so quietly, light on his feet. Like a butler – or a burglar? She was used to Alan's bold even step. Plenty of warning, there. Plenty of advance notice, the strong arm around the waist, the mouth closing over hers, sometimes leaving her nearly stifled. But she had to intuit where Jon might be. Although she might not turn, or leave her chair, she had to seek him out. And she felt he knew when she found him.

Did he arrive more often at the house, more often than the job would require? He appeared interested in her problems, certainly, but then he was being paid for that. Was he interested in her? Why did he ask those questions? What colour would she call her hair – toasted corn, but why would he want to know? Did he like children, or just her children? Asking would break the spell.

And that was what it was – just brain fever. Everything was so topsy-turvy, nothing seemed quite real.

The house was shrinking now. Room by room. In preparation for the tenants, Patsy was clearing the house of family idiosyncracies and preparing it for occupation. It had to be perfect, not just for the terms of the agreement, but because she wanted the incomers to see how good it could be. Couldn't bear for them to see its little uglinesses and inadequacies. The greasy fluff between cooker and wall.

She was remaining her usual bright, considerate self, her neighbours marvelled. Even with so much to do. You never felt she really needed any help – and anyway, she had more important people to organise things for her now. Which, in some ways, was what they had always suspected.

Alan's secretary, Margery, had typed the inventory lists, setting out their household possessions in satisfying columns from pocket-sprung divan with satin upholstered bedhead to bent metal toastrack. Margery was effusive in her willingness to help (anything for Mr Hopkins, of course), Patsy resolutely charming in her acceptance.

Fred Rookin rang daily. Or more often. His tone was increasingly familiar, larded with heavy, avuncular jokes. He didn't hesitate to use her Christian name and seemed not to notice when she retained his title. He praised her like a favourite niece, by marriage perhaps, adored and admired and perhaps a little more. On a couple of occasions, he invited her to events in the evening, but babysitting was hard to come by. Once, he persuaded a tense-lipped Margery to sit with the children for a few hours while he accompanied Patsy on a company trip to the theatre. In the round, which Patsy immediately declared her favourite type of performance. Well, well, declared Rookin to the assembled party, all couples from the firm, will the Americans be ready for our Mrs Hopkins and her progressive tastes? Reminds me, he said, of a definition I heard the other day. What's home cooking? The group tittered in anticipation. Something, declared Rookin, that a lot of wives of today aren't. An appreciative guffaw. No offence, Mrs Hopkins, he added, I'm sure you wouldn't take offence at an old fool like me. Patsy smiled, taking her usual place in the spotlight, but when the house lights went down she leant away from Rookin on the arm of her seat. Onstage, cradled between the rows of pointy-toed court shoes and gleaming brogues, an actor playing a Fleet Street journalist wrangled with his estranged wife and mother-in-law. The latest thing.

The ideal home is outstanding but not eccentric. It does very little different — but it does it better. The hostess knows that her guests will be immediately relaxed (and impressed!) by a spreading buffet. Wine, conversation and bonhomie flow together in easy moderation. Little touches, napkins folded like water-lilies, a bubbling soup, crusty French bread for that casual touch, perhaps with another continental import, a soufflé. Timing and precision are all. The rest should be so much fun.

Later she will forget who made the approach. The sequence of events will become inevitable. She will have no recollection of the effort it takes to invite him to stay for a drink before she collects Sally from across the road and the other children from various houses up the Drive, or the fortitude to ride out his embarrassed dilemma over accepting. At any moment she might have collapsed into polite rebuttal, no, no, of course not far too early, or too late. In retrospect, she will soften the strange clumsiness of her body against the fridge or the sink or the edge of the kitchen table as she moves around the room, busying herself with invisible tidying. Until then, she's only held his glance a little; nothing extraordinary. Nothing she can be blamed for.

But now there isn't much time and she is suddenly the petitioner. Her hand lies awkwardly on his jacket lapel, stranded between composure and disaster, between sophistication and gaucherie. She observes the hand, knowing it can move an inch either way. Almost out of curiosity, she lets it creep towards the inch of skin between collar and hairline. No thunderbolt descends. Somewhere in her inner ear, a voice is singing brightly, something Donald plays. Always true to you, darling, in my fashion; always true to you, darling, in my way. Perhaps if he kisses her, a torrent of feeling will sweep her along. And then she will have no choice.

He does. And she chooses to let go.

There is an area between hall and study, a small refuge from the open plan in which the turn of the stairs quite obstructs the view of the window. It is one of the few corners of the house where light has not yet been induced to fall. The darkness is alluring; it gives the area an excitement, like a deep cupboard in hide and seek.

Their noses bump. He strokes the side of her face, slowly, tentatively. The clock in the kitchen clicks by. The doorjamb cuts into her back. From the pale wood sideboard comes the scent of the green apples in the bowl. His eyes close to are watchful. She cannot bring herself to watch.

When she turns her head, Patsy catches a slice of reflection in the mirror: Evie's house across the close, where Sally is playing, moving the little stones on to the Fisons-fresh grass.

With an expression of troubled concentration, he moves his hand to rest on her hip. The lining of her skirt rustles. His hand drops; he raises it awkwardly to his own forehead.

"I don't understand," he whispers. "Please tell me. Why . . .?"

Into the shoulder of his jacket she sighs. How can she know? She can feel nothing and everything at once and the plastic ticking of the kitchen clock has juddered into stillness. Please don't ask.

He pulls back and looks at her, almost amused, searching her face for clues.

"No," he says, incredulous. "I can't . . . *you* can't. It's not . . . possible."

"No," she echoes, her voice flat. "It isn't." She pushes past him, smoothing down her skirt. She breathes deep and keeps her back to him. "I am terribly sorry. There's nothing else I can say. I made an awful mistake. So silly."

"No – well, yes. You did." He sounds as though he's gulping for air. "But it's my fault, too. I . . . must have . . . Well, *I'm* sorry. Please don't be angry."

She laughs her polite laugh, but she's trembling. "Please. It's forgotten. No need for an apology."

"But I am sorry." She feels him close behind her and the hesitant touch of his hand on her shoulder.

He takes one of her hands, turning her to face him. "It's a very hard time for you, I'm sure. All your life up in the air. And you must be missing your husband."

She smiles again, but this time, with more confidence and meets his gaze. "Yes," she lies. "That's it. All so silly, really."

8

THE LOGISTICS are a challenge – but Patsy has always proved good at challenges.

The children are passed among friends and neighbours like dancers in a reel. Under Evie's tutelage, Sally plants a tiny rock garden with a mirror pond. Her own little place is set regularly for lunch beside Donald at the polished dining table. How we'll miss you, darling, Evie breathes into the child's blonde curls when Patsy arrives, twice as bright and efficient as ever, to pick her up around five. Jimmy and Lucy find themselves making the most of the last days with their schoolfriends. If Mandy Martin collects them from school, they head off with the gang on their bikes down to the tree by the little river until the one with a watch notices the time, or someone comes yelling for them for tea. The gang discuss the concept of America for hours, and as they spin wheels on the muddy bank in imitation of the dustbowls of Arizona, Jimmy's swagger falters. Will Arizona be as impressive without the gang there to see it? Who will move into his place on the tree – some new arrival on the Drive with a facility for staying underwater longer than twenty-seven seconds and a six-blade penknife? Already nothing is the same. Lucy grows truculent. One afternoon, she kicks a boy so hard that a livid triangular flap of skin hangs down like a road sign on his shin. No way out, it says.

And twice Jon drives the two of them in the car to the office, for Patsy to complete the forms of her new privilege – power of attorney, or travel insurance. And once on the way back, as Gene Pitney, troubadour of divided love, squeezes out "Town Without Pity" on Mr Rookin's car radio, they divert to the lower road to the Hill where no one walks any more. So much easier to drive to the top and have the view unfold from the white-posted car park. Between the pines, a narrow zigzag path leads up to a sheltered clearing. Patsy's shoes slip on the needles and Jon takes her hand to keep her steady.

She's high on anxiety and anticipation, but he's almost playful, caught up in the moment. Frightened of her own pallor in the bright daylight, she curls under the tartan rug, while the sun catches the golden hairs on his skin, tanned by weekends cycling and walking. The danger – the *precautions* – the layers of extra risk weigh on her with a terrible excitement. They can't, can they? She clings to him, willing him almost to hurt her. She's embarked now on a journey of discovery and humiliation so momentous that there can, surely, be no way back; a journey bearable only if he crushes from her all knowledge of what she's doing.

Strangely, he won't comply. Jon bends over her, intent on her body and its responses. Patsy observes his absorption with surprise and then, with a shock, her own.

At first, she avoids the word. It's an awful thing that's happened, that's all – terrible, but God and Jon's discretion willing, not final. Just once, for an afternoon, part of an afternoon only. And they were careful in every way. As careful as the inventory they've compiled, with the help of Alan's secretary.

So careful, in fact, that it may not, she reflects, have happened at all. When she can sleep, which is not for long, she wakes convinced that exhaustion has planted some Technicolor phantasm in her mind. That afternoon is reduced to slices of sensation: the slippery crush of the pine needles on the hurried journey up the hill, the fear and pounding excitement, the vinegary smell of some tall weed crushed beneath them. After all, there was nothing wrong in a walk – even carrying the dense Black Watch rug from Mr Rookin's car boot. Nothing need happen. But then there is the memory of her legs, bent awkwardly to one side as she sat on the uneven grass. She could only look at her shoes. Shoes and dark trees surrounding the clearing and the almost white sky. And she flinches from the thought of his face when she could no longer avoid his glance, when he moved closer to kiss her. She tries to push away the ugliness of her fingers struggling to straighten her suspenders, the broken nail, the desperate strain of smoothing her skirt back down over her hips beneath the tartan rug, the way her lipstick had bled on to her cheek when she checked in the compact mirror, the awkward smudge of eyeliner. The lumps and bumps in the ground alarmed her, pitching her towards him with a rush. Over Jon's shoulder she saw stalks of cow parsley and the bobbing heads of dandelions. The browned lower branches of the firs reached out.

Not much better than savages, really. There, on the ground, in the open. Dots in the bright, wide open.

The next day, as she stands in the grocer's shop, she can make out beneath his shirt the curved shoulder of the proprietor's son as he reaches over for the soap powder. And again, she sees Jon bending slightly to button himself and trembles.

But there is something yet more shocking, something that the merciful scarcity of images can't disguise. Even with her eyes tight shut and her limbs caught between his knees and the harsh drag of the rug, it's there. Pleasure. The terrifying power of pleasure.

No one must ever know.

Besides, as Jon says over and over again on that afternoon, and later, no one would believe it. He can't believe it himself. He inhales her perfume every time she visits Rookin's office. Shalimar, the kind of information he retains. When he holds a door open for her now, their bodies fill the space where once decorum imposed swaddling bands. Through the partition wall, he can hear the rush of her breathing and the scrape of her nylons at the ankle as she crosses her legs demurely in the tub chair opposite Rookin's desk. It is, Jon says, beyond belief.

Jon is at the house to supervise the loading of things to go by sea, trunks containing winter clothes and non-essential effects. He is so pleased to see her, he says shyly, as they watch Jimmy's hand-painted initials on the cases roll up into the back of the lorry. He thinks about her every moment. He hopes she is all right, that she isn't angry with him. It's so important that she's all right.

For all the chaos, in and out, Patsy is apparently more than all right. She is pneumatic, inspired. Her body motors with energy, racing to keep ahead of events. Her hair is swept up. When the children come home in the afternoons, she sweeps them up too, one by one, with a whoop. With only three weeks to go, Patsy has refused to let her kitchen appliances travel ahead in the first consignment of trunks. So the children enjoy the fruits of the electric whisk . . . Nesquik milkshakes and meringues whipped into architectural fantasies, infused with her same energetic breeze. At the table they find toast cut into jokey shapes – sky rockets and cars. She frightens them a little, but since their lives have suddenly become busier than ever before, there's little time for them to reflect.

In the living room, the new fireplace has been hollowed out and plastered. There is dust everywhere, sticky red-pink dust that lies on every surface. Over the next few weeks, Patsy will find a tacky coating on the most unlikely items, even upstairs, and wrinkle her nose.

It's questionable whether it has provided a true focal point, in fact. The hearth isn't quite in the centre of the room, hardly at all really, but the section of wall where it's been inserted protrudes sufficiently for it to look unusual. If you go around the corner into Alan's study area, you can see it from there, too.

Well, that's done it, well and truly, the builder says, several times. No going back now. I wish you joy of it, Mrs Hopkins, he adds with a cautious laugh. From the living-room window, Jimmy sprays him with silent machine-gun fire all the way down the front drive and then turns to ask his mother, "Isn't Jon coming today?"

She shakes her head, seeing the little particles of plaster dance in the sunlight. "I don't think so, there's no reason in particular today. I can't think of one, anyway." Jimmy turns away with a slight shrug, disappointed.

The next afternoon Patsy collects the children from school. They make a little picnic on the grass at home with a cloth spread out under the apple tree. The cypress hedge encircles the garden. Patsy is solicitous, pressing them to take more sandwiches and to cut the huge shop-bought sausage rolls in two, if they can't manage. Around them, dahlias wave from their back row in the border, yoo-hooing over the dutiful begonias. Behind her sunglasses, Patsy watches the children: Jimmy has flung himself back on the warm grass with one leg bent up and she sees the sinews of his thigh reaching into the grey worsted of his school shorts. He is humming some indistinct chant, possibly warlike. Something more important, in any case. Lucy is cutting the sausage roll into tiny portions for negotiation with Sally in a shop game, in which the buyer had better beware. Tears threaten.

"Daddy should phone soon," she says to them all, but letting her gaze rest on Jimmy. "Maybe even today."

"Yes," says Jimmy grudgingly, rolling over to watch an ant crawl along a daisy stem, "I haven't told him about the long-jump." Jimmy has trounced his best friend with a half-inch of grubby sand. There is no more noble victory. Hannibal, currently preparing to scale the Alps with all those elephants, cannot – despite the Latin teacher's much-imitated hyperbole – hope to compare.

"Not long now, darlings," says Patsy and at the unshaded edge of her vision she sees Lucy wince. In front of them, the house rises in its candid pebble dash and bright brick splendour. The sun is a little lower now and the garden glows, reflected like a fringed pond in the picture window of the living room. The window frames are immaculate in white gloss. Inside, Patsy may have begun to dismantle their home into numbered boxes, but out here it's still perfect.

This afternoon, Patsy doesn't have the concentration to play the imagination game. They've run endlessly through the new house, the cars, the kitchen – a fridge you can walk into, Daddy promises – bubblegum, which Patsy considers common, and soda fountains. Through repetition, the dream has worn patches. No more crumpets or *Tales of the Riverbank*. Some of their friends may have moved away by the time they return. And they won't be able to have any pets there because a year (maybe two, but Patsy hasn't dropped that one on them yet) is too short and they couldn't bring Lassie home. And Mummy complains enough already about no one feeding the cat except her.

On other days, Patsy would pick at the remains of the picnic, guiltily gulping down the remains of the fish-paste rolls, flexing her toes and knees to compensate for the extra intake. Moment on the lips, lifetime on the hips. But today she's too jumpy to eat — the crusts look repellent, angular and absurd — and she sits with her heels tucked under her, smoothing down her skirt. The night before in the bathroom, she suddenly glimpsed her legs with the eye of a stranger. Her body feels prickly and strange; she wants to turn it inside out and bundle it into the twin-tub, pushing it beneath the soapy water with the wooden spatula.

On the way in to fetch more orange squash, her feet are scorched by the crazy paving on the patio. She catches sight of a squinting reflection in the kitchen window. Bleached by the light, she looks like a snapshot, but a snapshot of someone else. In photographs, Patsy is always bright, cheekbones catching the light, chin tilted up and a quarter profile turned to the lens. Now she looks flushed and scowling; the sun is hot on her hair, which has taken on a yellowish tinge, but her face is in shadow, its contours lost in a slight puffiness. Behind her the children are clear and small around the bright white and red tablecloth. She looms in the foreground, like a negative exposure.

Adulteress. There can be no right way to do adultery.

Ah, Patricia. Something was happening to her even then, before they all left for America, I think. You know, she was a little like spun sugar. There was her hair, of course, the way people wore it then, each strand quite perfect, not like all this naturalness, this taking pride in looking undressed. But she *was* perfect, you must appreciate that, almost perilously so. Every time one saw her, there was something better, something more of the moment. Or so it seemed to the people on the Drive, which I admit was perhaps not the most cosmopolitan audience. And her house too, like something from a magazine. I always think of it as her house somehow, rather than their house, perhaps because I remember those weeks – or maybe months – when Alan had already gone ahead.

What a spring and summer that was! We burst into space. I remember Donald told me off for saying that. Not "we" he said, "they". And in any case, he said, chickens and dogs and monkeys had been there first. But Gargarin was handsome as well as a pioneer, with beautiful even teeth like an American. And then Shepherd went up there also, and *he* looked like an Eastern European, and then I could tease Donald with his "we".

Patricia's kitchen, everyone said, was like a space ship. So streamlined and all those machines to help. Pretty soon, we thought, there would be no housework – a robot to do everything. And if there had been a robot, Patricia would have been the first to enslave it. She made sure that, money permitting, she always had the latest thing, all the new gadgets. It was a force in our corner of the Close. The government was testing "A" bombs, men were shooting into space and all these vibrations were somehow making their way to our little group of houses.

And even then I noticed this one funny thing. Across the road Patricia was trying to push forward in the world; but me, I was trying to hold back. Every morning I'd wake as soon as the curtains first began to get light and I'd lie there looking across at Donald with his hair all sticking up against his pyjama collar. And I'd think: "One more day, my darling. Just another day. Please God."

It's what happens when you marry late, and what's more, you marry someone so much older. And you know by then that nothing stays the same, good as well as bad, although we were lucky. We had good years. Not so many, of course, but good.

Patricia – for her it was exciting, and perhaps a little frightening, to have life stretch out way in front of her. When there's so much ahead, so much potential, you worry that you make the right decision, that you are going to do it all properly. And you know how spun sugar comes out in those little thin strands, the stuff a *patissier* uses to bind together a great mountain of *profiteroles*? I'm back to the spun sugar thing again, but indulge me with this, please, for a moment. Well, Patricia, she had a little cross, like two fine strands, just between her eyebrows. Not lines, she was too young yet for real lines, but a crease, a kind of refusal in the centre of that pleasing face.

I often thought, when I first knew her, that something had made her angry. It was partly Alan, perhaps. He was a darling, clearly. So enthusiastic, such energy and the children adored him. But he went away all the time, even when he was right there at home. Sometimes you could see him drift off, in the middle of a party, in the middle of a conversation, even if it was just you and him. Not exactly rude, of course; he was never rude, not intentionally, but he could be . . . absent. Some exciting project or plan. He loved to plan and, as it turned out later, he could really make those plans happen. Very successful man, Alan.

Patricia had plans, too. She wanted them to work together. I suppose by Alan's standards they did. But she was strong too, in her home – then. No woman likes to be a nag or a scold – I did enjoy scolding my Donald; it always made us laugh – but perhaps Patsy felt it was undignified.

As I say, she had everything that most of her neighbours aspired to. It seems funny now, but everyone then was jumping on the travelling staircase. Happiness on the HP. Funny how no one mentions the Hire part now.

I could never do that; I believe in saving for what you want. And waiting for it. More fool me, eh?

After a few days, Patsy no longer shrinks from the glare of the hillside. She's losing the sharpness of his distorted features. When she sees them almost daily in subdued, average light, in the kitchen, for example, or by the flat strip illumination of Mr Rookin's office, she can see that he is not threatening, whichever way you look at him.

If anything, he appears slightly vulnerable, although he's lost none of his spring. When she considers what they did, she's horrified, but also a touch intrigued. It's so extraordinary as to take on a fabulous quality. How could he know how to cut a path through her? He must hold some knowledge that no one else has divined.

And Jon remains charming and polite and amuses the children and, just occasionally, she'll catch him gazing at her, briefly, with an intensity that he defuses instantly with a quick smile. The reaction begins slowly, a drag on her legs like a weariness. At first, she puts it down to the shock and to a fear that she has done something shameful and stupid and destructive. It takes hold then, spreading into her lower back, stealing around her hips and reaching down and around between her thighs. Before she knows it, in the space of one afternoon as the children rush around them up and down the stairs and into the garden where the paddling pool sags on the lawn, she can feel her body swell and reach out across the forbidden space, singing to him to come nearer.

For now and for the next few days, she is his project. Everything she does, he notes. Her schedule, her finances, her dates and paperwork, her slightest preferences – in the

name of his employer he has to follow these. Then, going
where Rookin would scarcely dream, he records her
moods, her smell, the warmth or moisture of her skin –
even her cycle. She cannot dare to believe his interest.
Things she has striven to disguise or reform all her life
become central to his life. The world is inverted, turned
upside down, plunged into the vortex of the twin-tub.

He cannot, he says, keep away from her.

Those last few weeks, we saw a great deal of the children.
There was always someone coming or going from their
house and with so much upheaval it was easier for them
to make our house something of a base, you see. Not that
Patricia wasn't organized. Donald offered several times to
drive her to the office or into town, but she usually had
something arranged. I think the Company was very
helpful.

She did seem more than usually distant, though, a little
strained in our company. Donald noticed that she wasn't
as relaxed as she usually was with him. She would always
play to him a little, like a small girl, asking his advice.
Flirting, nothing serious, but like a clever daughter with a
favourite relative. Knowing she could do no wrong. I had
guessed, early on when we first knew her, that she missed
having a father of her own as she grew up. You could tell
that.

I teased Donald one day that he had been replaced in
Patricia's affections by the young man from the Company

who was so helpful with all the preparations. And so beautiful of course, the way some young men are with that healthy bloom, more demure I always think than young women at that age, who are so knowing. Flattering too, for Patsy, to have someone so eager to help, all that attention, not that Patsy lacked attention. Admiration, anyway. Mostly admiration from a distance.

At the time, I remember thinking they weren't leaving a day too early. That it was time Patricia saw her husband again. Although I knew we would miss them dreadfully.

9

IT IS as well that Alan's bed in Bettesville is so large because his nights are becoming as arduous as his days. At two or three in the morning he turns over his pillow, punching it into submission with a sigh, and seeks out the cool corner of the sheet with his foot. The new fibre has come through the tests splendidly on all the important indicators. Everyone is very pleased, particularly with the tenacity ratios. This yarn will not give up, wear out, change shape or otherwise betray its initial purpose. In the textile lab, they have already created a fabric of sorts in the usual porridgey hue. A test batch has been spun and lies coiled on a wooden skein like a mariner's rope. The pigment people are working on colour charts – Spaceshot Graphite, Mesa Verde (some smart-aleck Geography major came up with that for the green, but it will have to change), Walden Brown, Mooncloud.

Best of all, though, the fibre is tough, manly. What suits

the man on the road? Alanylene does. Praise descends on him, the limey chemist. Alan realizes that he is continuing in an honourable, if modest, tradition.

"After all," says Ray, when he buys Alan his umpteenth scotch ("The Antiquary" of Edinburgh), "we have the greatest respect for you Brits. As you know." And he proceeds to repeat the history. New York – London . . . Nylon . . . what greater monument to transatlantic scientific cooperation could there be? When this new fibre exceeds Terylene in high-class highly tailored mens-wear, they will have completed the circle, but there's no time to rest on their laurels (Alan's lost count of the number of times he's been told this, enough to have planted a whole new hedge, anyway). The opposition doesn't ease up.

At night, away from the reassuring glare of the lab, Alan does worry that there may still be tests worth running. Not the obvious: no one will get to wear this stuff without the closest scrutiny for reactions and allergies. No unpleasant rashes, anyway, or obvious abrasions of the skin. And it will never sag or possibly even wear out (although the men in marketing and personnel are becoming concerned about such durability, for obvious sales reasons). And Alanylene (he must stop this, but at night his brain whirls; it's close to unbearable) has fantastic adherent properties, so the colour will endure, too. There is nothing he can have overlooked, he consoles himself, turning his body at the waist so his legs hurdle towards one side of the bed while his torso turns the other, one arm flung above his head, his nose nestling in his armpit, redolent still of Odor-o-no.

When he wakes in the mornings now, adrenalin no longer propels him to swing his legs over the side of the bed even before his eyes are quite open. At first, he would sit there, swaying slightly, weighing the world and his place in it, clammy and feverish with nerves, before launching himself into the day. Now he gazes at the metal ring on the ceiling light – anodized, he guesses – and counts the little sepia shadows of dead moths in the plastic diffuser until the flux of urgency and dread equalizes in his endocrine system.

This morning he lies there a minute or two longer. Sunday. Ray and Marian have invited him for brunch, it goes without saying, and he will arrive around ten, driving himself cautiously in his new Plymouth. As he crawls along, he looks up at their house from the snaking approach road. A few weeks ago, it seemed the most casually impressive domain he'd ever encountered. Now he's begun to notice occasional signs of wear on the woodwork around those huge windows. A plume of pampas grass is bent over, decaying orange at the break.

On the terrace, Marian has assembled her usual triumph of gelatine, policed by pitchers of orange juice and coffee percolators. Trays of pastries glisten. To fortify him for this marathon Alan has taken the precaution of a couple of eggs at the hotel: he's abandoned the concept of soft-boiled after a series of misunderstandings, but is now accustomed to chasing what's called a four-minute egg without its shell around his plate. Has this great nation never imagined the egg cup? As he sits in the lounger, watching the sprinkler revive the sloping lawns, he muses that, by this time next week, he may well have the keys to his own new home which Patsy will colonize in her much-imitated style, much imitated in the Drive anyway. There'll be new models to emulate here.

When two more couples have arrived in a burst of greeting, Ray excuses himself and Alan from the company. Not more business, exclaims Marian, feigning despair, her hands resting on hips sculpted by stretch slacks. Be kind to Alan now, she winks. Alan grins back steadily. He indulges Ray a little these days, like an ageing beauty. Alan has started to glimpse life outside the conduit of Ray's enthusiasms.

Dick van Dyke, says Marian, it's Dick van Dyke. She puts a finger to her lips and scrutinizes Alan through half-closed lashes. Last fall, in one of their biannual trips to New York, she and Ray took in the new Broadway sensation *Bye Bye Birdie*. And that's it, she realizes now, it's been bugging her ever since she met him. But it *is*, the likeness is there, Alan to perfection. Alan beams back broadly happy with this enigmatic morsel. Oh, really?

In his den at the end of the house Ray fiddles with the blinds to filter out the intrusive sun. As Alan's vision expands into the gloom, he is assailed by the hundreds of images that jostle on the wall above Ray's desk and fan across the pinboard behind the couch. At first, he suspects a salacious theme. Ray and Marian are nothing if not frank and this might be a collection of exotica on open display. Gradually, however, with a contraction almost of disappointment, he discerns that it is nothing more than a mass of yellowing press cuttings and typewritten articles, fastened here and there with thumb tacks. By the side of the desk he notices box-files, the top one bulging with yet more paper. Ray clears a bundle of large envelopes off the seat of the couch to allow Alan to sit.

"So," says Alan, with a dreadful cheeriness, "what's all this then?"

"Alan," declares Ray, swivelling in the leather chair at the desk and stretching backwards until his legs lift off the floor, "this is my crystal ballroom."

"Future trends," Alan confirms, nodding appreciatively, perusing the faded headlines with greater interest. From the couch around him rises the scent of Ray's cologne. The air is warm: particles of dust drift in the bars of sunlight that persist through the blinds.

"Part of my job, Alan. Prognostication, knowing what tomorrow will bring, today. Take a look around."

"And what will tomorrow bring – brave new synthetic fibres?"

Ray laughs, as he does too often. Alan has known from the outset that Ray is an expert on the future, as he is on most things. Ray's glimpses ahead are at once invigorating and depressing to Alan who cannot imagine that the future in America could be any more fantastic than the present.

Anyway, Alan likes to find his way, logically. Leaps in the dark are not his style. But Ray's the boss, for now.

Ray is thrusting a leaflet under his nose, expounding a theory about work. Automation. Revolution in working patterns. A few hours a week, no more. Robots. Leisure time. The new renaissance, the need to find challenging pastimes.

Outside, Alan hears Marian laugh. How does someone so lively flourish with someone so glib? He looks across through the slats of the blind to the group outside. Marian's dark head is bobbing animatedly as she recounts some anecdote. Alan tries to imagine Patsy among these people; recently he's found that he cannot exactly recall her features and the photograph in his wallet is increasingly enigmatic. She sits there among the children in the living room, but her practised smile excludes him. He can imagine what she might do but not how she will look. He hopes she might laugh like that, tease him the way Marian does, but somehow he cannot imagine that either.

Ray is moving on to nutrition. A growing world population may mean some unfortunates won't be able to get their hands on a decent meal. And that means no trade, or less trade, anyway. The answer? Sacrilege to a beef-eater like yourself, Alan, but they could consider insects; termite ranching – termite eats the waste products, twigs and so on. Termite's a high-protein source. Beef in miniature.

Alan grimaces, which delights Ray. "I say, anything more palatable in view?"

"The oceans, Alan. Once again, within twenty years, by the 1980s, there'll be world government for the oceans, just as we're heading towards for the land. We need to begin farming those oceans, colonizing them."

"But don't you have enough land here, Ray?" Alan is beginning to feel a little impatient with these long-range fantasies. The near-future is more than exciting enough.

Ray passes Alan a typewritten screed. Its subdivisions are underlined in red which has bled a little on the thin copy paper. The red part of the ribbon is obviously in better condition than the black, Alan observes. He flicks through the pages, pauses at the dummy prospectus for the undersea hotel, where jet-propelled taxis ferry diners to the satellite restaurants. Ray's expression has intensified as he fixes his attention on Alan's reaction. Alan breathes in his cologne, stripping it down to its component layers. There's acetone, obviously, and musk and a mildly unpleasant rancid note, nut oil perhaps, possibly brazil. It's a trick at which he excels. He once rather successfully identified whale tallow in some new scent of Patsy's, gardenia he thinks: the warmth of her neck had vaporized the alcohol and the volatile oils and there it was. Fascinating.

Alan nods slowly. From the patio comes a strain of leggy dreamboat Ann-Margret; clearly progress also means you can dispense with surnames. She Just Doesn't Understand. He could watch her for hours. She could fix him with those wide eyes and pour out all her troubles. American women's predicaments are so much more charming and amusing than their British equivalent. They feel like adventures, not accusations.

Alan nods again, reflexively. Ray is staring at him once more, as if the Brain to Brain communication detailed in the torn cutting on the wall behind his cranium were already in play. In that glance, Alan sees the usual assurance and conviction that, as he clenches his buttocks to stare back, gives way to something altogether larger and more powerful. Ray's brown eyes are dilating with uncertainty.

A couple of weeks ago, a chat in Ray's study would have provided the essence of what Alan is here for: colleagues discussing the future of a great project. Alan's beginning to fidget, however. Ray is rather like a sleek fish, with Alan swimming along in his wake, but now he can make out bigger shapes in the water above him and he's becoming curious as to how it might feel to deal with them directly. A fortnight ago he would have been terrified but suddenly Alan feels a jolt of excitement that he might one day, in his own right, be up there with them.

"Fascinating, Ray," he forces himself back into the room. "But when will it happen? Is it really what people want?"

"What people want? Oh, everyone's after truth these days, Alan. That's a commodity to be in."

They lapse into acetone-tinged torpor. The orange wheels on the rug spin towards the door. Ann-Margret starts up again. So does Ray.

"Marian's sister, she lives out west on the coast, but she came to stay a while back. She was always on about something she'd read in some magazine. Cary Grant – around the time of that stuff (you remember? Well, I guess not) about him and his shrink and the lysergic acid. Something about being just a bunch of molecules until you knew who you were. Marian, don't get me wrong, she's devoted to her sister, but she said you could always spot the person who'd discovered themselves, because he or she was the one left alone after everyone else had left. Together."

Alan holds back a smile. "I expect the temperature in the room dropped by a couple of degrees after that."

"Well," says Ray, gazing down at his pudgy hands, "like I say. Sisters." He looks uncharacteristically subdued for a moment, then rallies. "Hey, you know the thing that impressed me about all this lysergic acid?"

Alan makes an encouraging sound.

"It's the speed of it. It delivers. If psychiatry can deliver truth, which I guess is what we're all after now – all of us, guys in business, men of science like you, Alan, government, whatever, then maybe this stuff can deliver it faster."

Alan shakes his head doubtfully, blowing out his cheeks, not buying Ray's reasoning, but wondering still about the structure of it all. Already, he's playing with the building blocks of carbon and nitrogen, the linking walls of hydrogen in the organic architecture of d–lysergic diethylamide . . . As it stands, it's a traditional house with an octagonal pool arranged around a series of courtyards. But if you could just take that wall down there and pair those two loose arms with . . .

Ray's drift is moving into more predictable waters. "Now, women. Alan, if we could only know what they really want . . .? We're getting more open here, more sophisticated, I guess . . ."

. . . and in that architecture Alan glimpses a parallel form that reminds him of something he's been staring at these past weeks. It's a disturbing possibility if he could only latch on to what it is, something he should have done or checked, perhaps, but Ray's cologne and the dusty warmth and the hiccupping of Ann-Margret in the light outside manacle his responses and push him back into the brown depths of Ray's den. Still, it leaves him feeling vaguely uneasy.

"Do you think that's right, Alan?"

Alan nods once more, furnishing his mouth with the kind of knowing smile he suspects the occasion calls for.

"Frankness, candour about sexual matters. That's the future – and we'll all be better for it." Ray smiles at him in a concluding way and takes a short breath. "So, Alan, progress is good, we're ahead of schedule if anything. Pretty enviable position to be in, huh?"

"I suppose so," Alan has cleared his throat and frowns in obvious concentration.

"Make us pretty popular guys. Within the corporation."

"Yes." Alan has had a series of meetings on his own with Mr Farebrother, whose tattooed head can glisten with enthusiasm, while his expression remains grim. He rarely looks at Alan directly, but Alan is heartened by his brusque manner and grudging endorsement. It reminds him of a schoolmaster he once had; it makes him feel he knows where he is, which has been a rare enough sensation over the past few weeks.

"And," adds Ray, "outside."

Alan is suddenly concentrating. Ann-Margret has retired from the turntable. The guests and Marian have drifted across the grass where the gurgle of their chatter is intersected every few seconds by the lawn sprinkler's swish. For the moment, he no longer wishes to be with them. Something is taking shape here.

"You mean recognition for the research department, Ray?"

"Sure. And specifically for the authors of the project."

"Well, that would be nice, I suppose. Gratifying."

"Very gratifying. People in the business think a lot of you."

"I doubt that," Alan squirms on the dark weave of the couch. "They can hardly know who I am. You're the public face of the Innovative Fiber Department."

"Oh, they know, believe me. I know they know."

"Do you? How . . . would that come about?"

"It's as well to know the competition, Alan. I keep an eye on them and they keep an eye on us."

"Ah." Alan suspects there's a question he should be asking here, but he is suddenly paralyzed by embarrassment or reluctance. There's something in all this he's not quite ready for. A decision ahead, some response that he has not yet had time to synthesize. Ray smiles at him and hums a refrain. Put on a happy face.

"I suppose I *can* see it, Alan. Dick van Dyke – the long legs, the scholarly air, the quiet charm with the women . . . yes, there *is* something. So, tell me, Alan. If you had to choose between Eva-Marie Sainte and Audrey Hepburn and Sophia Loren, what would you do? Or do you prefer the Novak type? Maybe you do."

Alan shrugs helplessly, putting his hands up, defeated. Outside, there is a burst of laughter, a scuffle and a shriek and then the static tear of needle across vinyl. A new rich voice flings out like a lariat. Alan recognizes it because Marian played it for him the last time he was here. Over a jaunty bass-line, Patsy Cline falls to pieces each time she hears his name.

"Here, see this." Ray reaches behind him to the desk and slides out an open book which has lain beneath the tobacco-coloured piles of cuttings. "Now here's a futuristic dream. It's a bunch of – what do they call them . . .?" he swivels the volume to look at the cover, ". . . 'partly-baked ideas' and this, Alan, sure is underdone."

"*Immortal Art*" Alan reads, "by I. J. Good . . . What is this?" Ray gestures for him to read. It's something about records. He and Patsy only have a modest collection; in his student days jazz was the thing, but he never really stopped to acquire much. These days they're too busy to spin discs. He tries to concentrate on the print. Something about recordings deteriorating because of the way they're recorded. If they weren't analogue but discrete, digital, they would spring anew with each copy. And what, Alan wonders, would be the point when there's been such heavy investment in disc–pressing technology? Who would need to replace records? Anyway, choice is what people want now, novelty. They'll hardly be going back to the same old recording again and again.

"Did you understand that?" asks Ray, grinning. "Is it possible?"

"Endless performances? Theoretically, yes. Logically most things are possible. But it's just a notion, the rational pushed to the ludicrous, Ray. You know I've plenty of time for the academic notion, but there's no call for this one. Let's stick to our synthetics; I reckon that's where the future lies." It's the first time he's contradicted Ray and he knows he sounds petulant but he wants to get out of this room and back to the sunny terrace and Marian's laugh.

"Sure, Alan, you're the scientist. Whatever you say."

10

IN FILMS, sophisticated women dawdling around thirty often dine alone. It imparts an air of intrigue or competence: the heiress, the newspaper reporter or the jewel thief all sip their aperitifs and tip their cigarettes at a table for one. At the Tudor Rose restaurant and tea room, however, women make a treat of coffee for two, reparation for the morning's errands and provisioning. Only a handful sit alone, mostly over fifty, apart from the occasional businesswoman.

Patsy is dressed for business in a navy three-quarter-sleeved dress, and a charm bracelet which lends authoritative weight to her left wrist. She is shown to a table by the window, with a view down into the High Street and a cool perspective of the rows of little tables perched on the red paisley carpet. The old timbers of the floor distort the composition. On the tables, menu cards incline at drunken angles.

It has taken an effort of will to climb the narrow stairs from street level into that labyrinth. The entrance is so narrow, the force inside unknown.

At a quarter past eleven, the Tudor Rose resonates with talk and the chink of cups. Heads bend towards each other in groups of two or three. Steam emanates from an urn on a dark wood sideboard, shooting the odd indiscreet hiss. Patsy orders coffee and biscuits from a freckled young waitress, but keeps her eyes on the desk by the entrance where the head-waitress sits reconciling orders and accounts. From time to time, she rises to greet a new patron and usher them to their table. Patsy watches her lift her head slowly as new feet nudge on to the swirling carpet, sees her broad back angle forward, observes the practised curve of her dip around the desk, the measured smile, the small inflection of her hand.

Jon has said so little about her. She is called Anne, but he hardly uses her name. Patsy feels he might be superstitious about it. The wedding is set for September, somewhere in north London. She can tell, try as he may to suppress it, that he is excited about the event, that her parents' arrangements impress him. The reception will be held in a hotel whose owners are friends of his fiancée's family. His suit is already waiting in his mother's spare room. Sundays are dedicated to trips to the future in-laws in Enfield. These journeys will be easier in the winter, when they have taken delivery of the car that Anne's parents have promised for a wedding gift.

Anne stands overseeing the trays that pass from the kitchen serving hatch. She straightens a doily or mops an overspill of frothy milk. Patsy sees her own waitress stop and exchange a word shyly with her superior. The older woman touches her briefly on the elbow and smiles. The younger one colours with diligence, frowning down at her tray.

Patsy stares at the long face; it puts her in mind of an illustration from the thirties. The legs in their dark stockings are straight, lacking definition. There is something on her jawline, some irregularity, a mole probably, that emphasizes the heaviness. No figure to speak of. Good hair, though, if rather severe in that classical twist, and good eyes, but nothing made of them. Not cheap, certainly; not insubstantial either. Stately, almost. Patsy looks away, frowning down into the street.

"Madam," the freckled waitress interrupts her view to lay down the china coffee pot and the cup. A small metal jug of steaming milk is placed at an angle. Three biscuits fanned out on the doily. Patsy reaches out her hand to the pot. At her wrist, the little Eiffel Tower that Alan bought her in the South of France trembles across the tiny starfish from Cornwall and the Egyptian cat he brought to the hospital after Sally's birth.

You have lovely things: Jon repeated the obvious like a caress. Lovely taste. She smiled indulgently at the observation but she didn't want his views on decoration; it levered open a chasm between them, one that scares her, as if there isn't enough to worry about already.

He's been to the house now, once, after dark.

Even years later, she will not believe it of herself or of him. He calls her at a quarter to nine. Shortly after she picks up the phone, Jimmy erupts down the stairs, swinging on the banister finial. Is it Dad? Whistling away his disappointment, he retreats.

Jon is not at his car maintenance evening class. Or at least, he could still be there for the second half, once the green cups and saucers have been cleared from the trestle tables in the village hall, if not for another possibility which neither of them wants to be the first to articulate. On his scooter, it would take maybe fifteen minutes. A quarter of an hour. Just to see her. He could get into the garden from the footpath that runs along the back. He's thought about it.

Jimmy, though. She worries that Jimmy will still be awake. Once he's asleep the Martians could land and he'd be cheerfully oblivious, but he's just run downstairs. Can she telephone him back? No, but Jon can try again in five minutes. Go for a walk around the block, keep unobtrusive. Perhaps he'll just ride over towards the Drive and find a box nearer the house. No problem if he has to turn back. But he does so hope he doesn't.

After a couple of minutes in which the silence in the house forces itself into her ears, she slowly climbs the stairs. Jimmy and Lucy's door is open a couple of inches and she pushes it gently. Lucy's end of the room is dark but this side of the partition the light from the pigskin shade falls on to Jimmy's table and the papier-mâché Saxon longbarrow he has crafted this term. Jimmy is asleep already, a book folded around his arm, one page crushed. She removes it, flattening out the leaf and places the book gently beside the glass of water on his bedside cabinet. As she switches off the light, he emits a drowsy affirmative sound, just to let her know, just like his father.

She sits by the telephone, fluttery and breathless, with cold fingertips. She waits for the short hiatus before the ring, the hiccup of anticipation. She snatches up the receiver.

A membrane is forming in the centre of the jug of milk. The biscuits are untouched. The head-waitress makes her stately progress between the tables, the front desk and the servery. Patsy fears her coming closer, her weight and substance, some scent she might recognize from the most subtle impregnation of Jon's skin.

Anne has two Siamese-cross cats, Lucy and Ricky, which he points out is all wrong, because, in this feline duo, it's Ricky who's the redhead. Jon enthuses about the cats, their antics as kittens, the little habits they've developed over the years. She knows he is looking forward to living full-time with their mischief and surprising turns of affection. He talks of things he and his fiancée do together, but never directly of Anne. On the few occasions when she has asked any questions (how did you meet? How old is she?) his face becomes tense. The answers are short. At a dance. Thirty-three. He is twenty-five.

Patsy catches herself imagining Jon teasing the cats in the flat that will be his marital home – once he's rebuilt the breakfast bar, retiled the little balcony and replumbed the bathroom. Siamese blood must give them wide cheekbones, she surmises, so the three of them can romp about displaying their bone structure. Jon's bones are Slavic, like that Russian dancer who's leapt the barricades in Paris, and all for love – a frame for those eyes. She sees the little toys, felt mice and fluffy pom-poms on string, lying about the floor. And Anne's indulgent gaze. Or worse still, all four of them, all twelve feet up on the settee, dozing to the sound of the Dansette.

The flat will be clean but beige, with gas fires in ugly old fireplaces. But then, there's been a deal of work done to it, and Jon's taste is clearly superior. Just look at his clothes, not expensive but with those little details. Elastic-sided jodhpur boots, not the average office wear. The flat might be functional but stylish. Flair on a budget. She looks at the back of the head-waitress's dark head and the hands, can discern from this distance that Anne (although Patsy also doesn't like to give her the intimacy of a name) is indeed wearing only the one ring and no varnish. When she stands up, it's possible that the black uniform might boast a slightly dropped waist, a touch of Gigi, which makes her dark appearance altogether more unsettling.

Finally, this woman with the flat pumps and the

elongated dress that could, it now occurs to her, be the height of jazz chic in some Parisian dive swings into the narrow thoroughfare that runs past the window tables. Her eyes check the state of cups and plates. She sweeps up a silvered tray emptied of *langues de chat* and suddenly, she is there, beside her. Patsy's pulse lurches.

"Can I get you some fresh coffee, madam?" she enquires, inclining towards her to hook away the cold pot. Her eyes, which must be hazel or brown, connect only for a half-second with Patsy's own. "And a fresh cup, perhaps?" noticing the muddy fullness. "Everything all right?"

Patsy nods, blushing – strange sensation for her – inarticulate. Her voice struggles out thin and regal.

"Nothing else, thank you. Just the bill."

The head-waitress smiles acquiescence and indicates the slip of paper on Patsy's table by the metal vase with its artificial carnation. "Whenever you like, madam. Please don't hurry. The desk is by the door."

From the leaded windows, she can see down into the High Street. The ruby glow of the apothecary's flask over the portal of Boots The Chemist reminds her of the prescription for Lucy's asthma medicine. At the mock-Tudor gents' outfitters, Jimmy's new blazer awaits collection. Haircuts at the department store, medical certificates from the doctor's surgery, a thousand adjustments and alterations to the launch module.

Back at street level, she is shaking and nauseous. One Patsy greets acquaintances in the street, smiling and chatting the same little routine. Just a fortnight to go. Yes, very exciting. Children make friends so quickly, don't they? All arranged for us over there. Very lucky, yes. No, we won't forget our friends here, no fear of that. No fear. The other Patsy shrinks from eyes that might burn into her back from a first-floor window. A look of hatred or worse, scorn. Or pity. But pity for what? A few minutes between two people, snatched here and there, private time locked in a secret pact.

Sometimes she cannot believe her secret, a gem in the most discreet setting, gleaming just for her. Sometimes she cannot believe that for the sake of a few minutes she has tainted her life. Occasionally, as Alan's wife, she glimpses herself as a stranger, and is horrified by the cold audacity of her behaviour. After what she has done, how can she chat with people in the High Street and collect asthma medicine from Boots – even notice that pink blouse in the window? It's unbelievable. Sometimes she knows that no one will ever know her better than Jon; that only in his eyes can she luxuriate and scintillate – expand and display – as she was meant to. And soon it will be over, her firework spectacular.

She sleeps little, turning to bury her nose in the pillow, imagining the grassy scent of his back, trying to block out the solid tobacco and soap undertone of Alan. One night Lucy creeps in, breaking the own-bed rule, snuffling from a nightmare. Patsy is glad of the diversion and the child crawls in gratefully and lies on her side with her back to her mother, Patsy's arm under her neck. Patsy strokes the child's upper arm languorously, enjoying the association of her tender skin – but it's not the right kind, it has little bumps from eczema and poor circulation. There are no muscles to give the flesh texture and definition. Lucy feels her mother's eyes wide in the dark behind her, her restlessness punctuated by a sudden tight embrace. Soon Lucy slips out and pads back to her own bed.

In the gleaming blue of night, Patsy makes an audit of the room. The left side of the built-in wardrobe, dresses, blouses and skirts in rainbow order; the right, Alan's suits and shirts, much depleted now, his winter overcoat already packed, assorted shoes and galoshes. These effects are intrinsically hers as well as his. She knows the creases on the shoes' faces; she recalls the colour thread she used to sew the buttons back on the coat, and when she did it. The moth sachets were laid in the shelf corners in late April. They're about due for replacement, but that won't be necessary now. The parade of concerns is so engaging, so involving, that it takes on the momentum of passion. This is her life, and she's proud of it. She's proud of her husband too, proud of their future, but she cannot overcome this frozen core, cannot shake herself out of this anger. Why can't she melt for Alan as she does in the arms of a stranger?

While the Drive sleeps, Patsy looks out of the window at the dots of landing lights left on. While she's away, not there to keep it up to scratch, the house will lose its lustre.

It will become like other people's homes, full of sometime modish installations that yellow and apologize for their stiffness in later years. Already, with some of their possessions en route to Bettesville, the house looks awkward. She begins to see how small the hallway is. The conformity of the shell shows through. Not so very different from all the others, after all.

It was she who was special. Now she has become extraordinary, even dangerous; she will probably never sleep again. She waits to engulf the next day.

The next day Lucy struggles with her reading. Janet and John do not set off down the wide path for her. The Shoemaker and the Elves (even with "sew" and "bought" and "already" highlighted above the text for special consideration) cannot fulfil their nocturnal pact. Strips of leather remain unsewn on the bench.

Patsy sits with her after school, her arm around her daughter's waist. Lucy tenses in her encounters with The Beacon Readers. Periodically, she asks Patsy if they can't read instead from the *Picture Dictionary*. But, sweetheart, protests Patsy, you can do so much better than that now. You're nearly seven, you're on the second Beacon Reader. Lucy frowns and reaches still for the dull red volume where dark boys with shiny cowlicks and wheat-haired girls with soft waves wear berets and gloves. But Lucy, Patsy persists, it's so old-fashioned. Lucy likes the rhythm of the repetitions, however, the flexing of each word's meanings. Everything on the table is out of order. Could you put the table in order? Spot obeys Jack's order. Jack keeps Spot in good order. He brushes and looks after Spot, in order to keep him well. Mother goes to the shop to order things.

Lucy murmurs the text to herself, sticking over certain illustrations, pondering the precise disarray of the blue and white cups and saucers on the check cloth or the curious illustration of Mother combing her long hair. No mother she knows has long hair, or if they do, it's neatly folded away from discussion. This picture shows the frank untidiness of the illustrated Mother's locks, normally pinned up. They have a strange fuzzy texture, like the dog, Spot. Mother looks at the same time older and younger and strangely engrossed, like a squirrel, in her grooming concentration. Lucy pauses in her articulation.

"Oh, come on!" sighs Patsy, snatching the book away, feigning playfulness, snagging her bracelet on a strand of Lucy's hair. "You've read this a thousand times, Lucy darling. Let's get on with the reading you're supposed to do, shall we?" When she hears the edge in her own mother's voice, Lucy looks down and sideways. Patsy feels a giddiness descend; all this practice and so little progress. How will Lucy fare in an American school, where everyone talks so fast? The stupid little English girl. But she isn't stupid, is she? Just stubborn sometimes. Patsy hasn't done a very good job with her, she's afraid. She can't remember a time when she looked at either of her daughters without being stung by a pressing need for improvement.

Elsewhere Patsy excels at cinnamon loaf or napkin origami or retouching the roots of her hair. In fact, it's close to miraculous the amount she is achieving. There has even been time to drop in on Mandy Martin for coffee. This will be one of their last encounters, Patsy knows. Rather earlier than anticipated Mandy is about to disappear from the story. For now, Mandy ascribes her friend's guardedness to her imminent ex-pat status, but Patsy also has her secret which she wraps around her like a see-through mackintosh. Still, they can chat away, socially grooming like a pair of clothes-conscious marmosets.

At the core of her days now there is one thing, one good thing. Jon is just perfect, so kind and thoughtful. He treats her like a goddess. He understands how intensely she feels; he doesn't talk to her as though she were some prize retriever or the bright young laboratory technician. She could never have believed a man could want so much to please a woman – and without all that hand-kissing compliment business that screen cads (and Fred Rookin) do, the attention that makes you feel blown up to ridiculous proportions, a target like a barrage balloon.

Her only regret is that he's become saddled so young, and with a waitress. He'll never reach his potential once she has her hooks into him. Lucy stumbles over "sewed" for the fifth time in as many minutes: Patsy lets it go.

Laboriously, the elves creep out into the workshop. Patsy slips back a little into the sofa, slipping off her shoes. Just supposing (and who knows what the future is bringing? – whatever you're not expecting, that's for sure) but just supposing they return in a year or so and the children will be that much older, with Sally about ready for kindergarten and so Patsy will have a little more time and maybe by then Jon will have left the firm to set up that business he talks about and perhaps, just perhaps, she might in some way, with her flair, be able to help, just as a friend of course because they do have this special understanding she and him, they'll always have that and they could meet just now and then, nothing special, just a chat, maybe a little trip for lunch somewhere, nothing anyone could blame them for (and anyway, who would know?) and no one would be hurt and she could feel the way she feels now at the prospect of seeing him tomorrow, even if only for a few minutes, because when he's there, life is simple and sudden and good.

A little before they left, I called by with an invitation to lunch on Sunday. There were so few opportunities left before that silver bird scooped them up and deposited them across the Pond. And Donald and I would miss the children so, especially Sally, the little monkey.

She was all in yellow, very bright. It's funny how you remember these things, even what I was wearing, those ridiculous Capri pants. Some illusion I had then with no height and a tendency to put on weight. Madame Michelin, Donald would call me when I was all wrapped up in winter; you know, like the advertisement. We were talking about the new house in America and a little about Alan's job, but that was always rather a mystery to me. Exciting, though, it had to be exciting, with Alan already there preparing the way. I knew she must like all that. To be moving on to the next stage. To be ahead.

Although that afternoon I remember I noticed that, for once, Patricia did not seem to be ahead. When I arrived, I had the sense that she had been wandering. Usually, she was so full of purpose, but this evening she was like someone rehearsing a play. Through the open window – it was still light, of course – I thought I even heard her murmuring to herself, as though she were rehearsing a scene in which she presented the emptying house to another person, somebody she seemed to like and know but who didn't maybe know the basic facts of her home life. This makes no sense, does it? But I fancied she was describing to someone (a friend? herself?) her everyday existence. Did she say something about wallpaper? About the one in the bathroom that Lucy called Sleeping Beauty's Briars? Or about the sofa where Sally said her first word?

I don't know now, maybe I'm exaggerating. I do wonder; it seems unlikely. But, I must tell you, I did have the impression that she was rehearsing scenes from her family life. Stations of the cross, no, I don't mean that – that will be an extra Hail Mary or two this week, for my sins. But here is the place where I listen to the children reading and so on, this is where we serve tea and the family relax here before bedtime. You know. An audience, it was as if she had an audience. But an audience in this case, I think, of just one. But who?

This sounds strange, I know. But it was almost as if she were sleepwalking. She seemed otherwise normal, if a little pale, but she had so much to do. Of course I was intrigued and I wanted to know how she was, how she really was. I know I can be too direct sometimes for English people. And I go on too long – my questions are endless. Poor Patsy – sometimes maybe I asked the kind of questions that she would have avoided even from her own mother. Especially from her own mother. She just slid away and down from anything I asked, so we went back to that safe subject, the future.

I wanted to know what her plans would be, after the new American house, would she start work on Alan's American superiors. I could imagine her being very help-ful as wife to a company executive. Oh, plans, she said. She didn't have plans: she just wanted to get the children settled into school. I didn't believe that, naturally; a person like Patricia is not happy without plans.

And then, I think this is right, she asked about the kind of plans Donald and I made. Were they for holidays, or trips to the theatre, plants for the garden? She was joking, I suppose, but she seemed almost desperate to know. Did we ever run out of plans? How could I explain to her that we were frightened of plans, that they were just a tempta-tion to fate? I made some joke back about not being organized enough. Just ferry tickets to the Continent, that was about as far as our plans went.

But she still wanted to know if we had rules and goals. Whether we divided life into who does what. She said it made her happier to have rules like that. She laughed, but not as far as the eyes.

Well, the only rule was to be sure you both wanted to do something, I thought. She asked if that was because marriage can be a long sentence. Something like that, although I don't think she used quite those words.

And then I had to say it. Yes, of course. But the strange thing, Patsy, is that for some of us, even a long time would not be nearly long enough.

She nodded then as if she understood, but for a moment I think she saw long empty corridors stretch out before her. For a moment maybe she didn't want new plans; she wanted her husband's arms around her. I suppose.

"I hope," she suddenly said, her cheeks pink like a little girl's, "that Alan and I will be as happy as you and Donald in thirty years' time."

It was so sweet; I had to smile, but even as I did, I thought — who else could be as lucky as we were? But I didn't say that. I said something reassuring, something like, "I'm sure you will, if that's what you want; you both seem very determined."

"Is that what it takes — determination?" There was a silence; from the kitchen, the Light Programme was waltzing away. And then she indulged me, like asking her grandmother for a favourite story. It was late and we'd drunk some of the sherry in that bottle she'd only have to

throw out in a few days anyway. "How did you and
Donald meet?"

And how could I resist?

11

FOR SOME reason, the laboratory had chosen Moon-cloud. Perhaps it was topical with the space shots, seasonal for the weather, touched with romance or simply practical, a weave of three batches of yarn, in dyes specially formulated in the laboratory by the pigment boys under the grudging supervision of Strachan, Petersen and di Stefano.

It was all the same to Alan, which colour they chose. He wasn't concerned with hue; he scrutinized the folds of the suit as it nestled in tissue in the box in front of him. Contour under stress, texture and surface – these were the acute issues. And would the fabric stay matt, but with that slight sheen to mimic lanolin?

The tailors had been sharp and fast. The cut was modish. Ray's little joke, another of Ray's little jokes, to have it made for him, to dress him, the scientist, overnight like a magazine mannequin. Still, it was only fair, Alan supposed, to put his body where his mouth was, as it were; only sporting that the people who would be actually manufacturing the things should see an example walking and talking before them. In any case, the style wouldn't be considered so extreme here. They'd simply put it down to ill-judged northern peacockery.

As they'd driven into North Carolina, he'd seen the swing-seats and rocking-chairs on the front porches. America hadn't so far disappointed, only exceeded. Everything was at least as big and as colourful as he'd ever expected. The rest of the world would never catch up. Nowhere could ever be like this.

Cool air in the car had kept them insulated until they stepped out at the formidable hotel in Raleigh. Then he felt his shirt slam into his back with the force of the night. The walls rose steep above the white portico; he saw a fire escape, like a diving board, outlined against the dusk. Pretty hot, the man at reception conceded, and humid with it. My wife says a woman in the post office today, she pressed the stamps to her hair before putting them on to the envelope.

In his room, he pulled back the pale drapes, hooking them into ornate gilt fixings, a little rusted. He tugged at the metal chain to extinguish the central fan light, the better to gauge his surroundings. Between his arrival and the first floor, thundery rain had begun, stones dropping. Against the flashing sky he saw the silhouettes of trees, tall with feathered foliage, racing each other upwards. He could make out a central square, some railings and vine-covered colonial buildings to the left. He leant his forehead against the glass. It wasn't cold. For an instant he saw the children in their pyjamas, regretted the orange glow of the living room and longed for Patsy's deft turn in the kitchen. Three thousand miles away he heard his own enquiry. What's for supper, then?

The porter had left the box on the end of the tall mahogany bed. It sat there, magenta tape crossed formally over shiny grey cardboard which bore the swirling legend "Your Suit, Sir".

His suit. He lifted it from the box. The shoulders angled obligingly; the trousers kicked down into the air. The smell of the laboratory lingered still, strange that, an aura of fluorescent strips and late nights. He wouldn't try it on tonight though, too hot, too tired. Instead, he'd let it doze in the panelled wardrobe so it could shed what little crease it had suffered. In the morning, when he'd showered, they'd both be fresh and ready.

The dining room was surprisingly well attended. Ray signalled to him from a corner table, away from the harpist. Alan slid into the chair opposite, pouring himself chilled water from the jug. Ray's neat hands cradled a tall glass of iced tea.

"Cocktail hour, Alan? Welcome to a Methodist state."

"Of course. I suppose it is. I don't mind at all, it's too hot anyway. My head's swimming already."

Ray put a hand to his mouth, mock conspirator. "I've got a little bourbon in here. Want some?"

Alan shook his head, smiling back, and looked around,

unsettled by the occasional wave of a nagging scent he couldn't identify. It had been strongest near the door, but it was still finding him out, sweet and sinister. At the next table, a middle-aged woman in embroidered silk laughed decorously at her neighbour's witticism. As she turned, Alan saw the green-veined white bloom at her breast, and another pinned to the flushed young woman at the table across to his left. He could distinguish them now around the tall dining room, moonglow twists on black lace collars and demure fichus, sly luminous winks on wired evening bodices. Looking back towards the door, he saw the mahogany tray of flowers and the maitre d' poised to bestow them upon the lady patrons. The scent lingered in his nasal passages; he found himself gulping mouthfuls of air.

"You know," Ray was saying, "those tea cups probably have fancy French wines in them. When people dispose of their liquor bottles round here, they wrap them in newspaper – got the neighbours to consider. Anyways, I reckoned you wouldn't mind if we ate here tonight. Tomorrow we have a full schedule. There's the factory tour at Zebulon – the discussions about specifications, your kind of expertise, Alan – then in the evening, there are some people I'd like you to get to know. That's my kind of skill. But we'll meet them someplace else. One night here is enough . . . Tomorrow night, however," and Ray twisted the Pepsi bottle, following its glass striations with his manicured finger, "tomorrow – 'take me to Havana'."

The road to Zebulon curved and dipped between groves of green. It swooped over little streams and snaked up broad reaches of galloping pointy-leafed weed. Red-fronted birds with long tails bobbed along branches above them. Pink crepe myrtle bushes waved at their car. Tobacco fields reached to the tanning sun. Even at seven-thirty, the air was syrup. Zebulon, halfway between fabled city and synthetic fibre.

"Paradise, Alan?" enquired Ray, already behind dark glasses. "Well, you just wait." Despite the early coffee, Alan was struggling to keep awake. Zonked, said Ray, you look totally zonked. Oh really? Alan murmured. The air-conditioning in the car, which had seemed more than adequate on the drive down, was struggling too. It huffed and sighed from the giant grilles on the dashboard. The driver frowned and made tiny adjustments to the controls. Ignoring Ray's admonitions, Alan wound his window down to get the breeze. Shrugging his shoulders, Ray did the same. The hot air buffeted them past the roadhouses and timber yards and on past the angular lights like giant lilies over the gas pumps.

Ray and the driver shouted observations to one another. Tobacco auction time of year; people round here talking of little else. Fine place, but for the bugs. Could you stand the bugs? Not me. And now they'd had to stop the DDT spraying around some of these parts, because people complained about chest problems. Would you believe it. Only a few days, but they'd have to be careful.

Unless they were real vigilant, bugs could destroy everything. Nature didn't take no prisoners.

Alan began to calculate the speed of the car with the coefficient of wind. If they had to stop at that crossroads, would it be for five or ten seconds? Dredging up his school physiology, he tried to recall the human cooling mechanism, to understand when the sweat glands would pump out, bringing relief to the overstressed epidermis and mutinous internal organs. But it was too hot to pursue that thought.

The turning to Zebulon was wide, dominated by a pale green water tower, an H. G. Wells monster with a swollen belly, boasting the town's name in rust-red paint. The avenue was flanked on one side by a square redbrick mansion with yellow stucco porch, presiding over green lawns and regimented beds. On the other, respectable villas adjusted white gloves for the arriving visitor.

They crawled into the main street. Glancing sideways, Alan saw there was little more, beyond a couple of intersections which petered out after a few hundred yards. Antoine's Department Store announced its July Sellathon in discreet lettering. Alan hoped they wouldn't stop in the inconsiderate sun, but the driver needed precise directions. Left or right, darned if he knew.

Trying not to breathe too deeply, for fear of raising his heart rate, Alan felt the collar of the suit, which bent slightly to his touch, but retained its cool, waxy texture. Ray had bounced out into the heat and poked his head into the soda shop, exchanging a few comments with the men in the window booth. He rolled on up the street a little way and back, whistling.

On they drove, swinging a wide U in the street and turning right down the first intersection, signposted Rockymount and Hobgood. On past the clutch of new houses built around a farmstead, on until scrubby forest spread out on their left and low windowless brick buildings stretched fingers into the green on their right. First a timber yard, then a mattress manufacturer, then Heavy Hog Dungarees, with its smirking, snorting, stampeding logo and then, furthest out, the name barely visible on a sunburst of yellow paint, Cassandra Textile Mills.

"Okay," said Ray, and he clicked his knuckles. "Okay then. Let's see what they have in store for us."

The entrance hall to Cassandra Mills was panelled in a dejected wood whose varnish had blistered in the heat. The smell of adhesive lay on air cooled by a large metal cabinet; its exhalations barely stirred the leaves of a dusty cheese plant. When he had stopped simply being grateful for the cool, Alan could take in the photographs of some local dignitary shaking hands with representatives of the mill. No one smiled.

Ray was bending into a window in the panelling and, even from where he was standing, Alan could tell that air-conditioning did not permeate this little cell. In it were two women, at the front the elder in a ruched pink daydress and pink lipstick, powder clinging to the lines around her mouth. Behind her, at an angle, sat a tall Negress, occupied in some clerical task. Alan could only see her quarter profile; her lips moved gently, checking column against column.

The pink woman was all attention. They were expected. She enunciated a list of the various senior figures within the company who would arrive within instants, if they would be so kind as to accommodate themselves in the intervening period in the waiting room, which they should find moderately comfortable as the air there had been acclimatized.

Alan watched the woman behind her stand to carry a ledger across the little room. She was tall, maybe more than six feet. She moved like a girl, her long dark dress swinging around her calves, but where the Alice band dug its teeth into her hair at the temples, a wave of creamy white pushed back the dark. As she turned, he saw the twists in her plaited bun. She caught his glance, held it for a leaden instant, and dropped her eyes back to her work. Alan felt hot, nettled, defeated, unnecessary and full of adolescent admiration.

Unlike Ray, who was practised in the art of repeating and retaining new names, Alan fumbled them all. He sipped his iced tea as the managing director delivered welcoming homilies. He loped along in the group, fighting the urge to yawn, as their hosts levelled a fusillade of facts about Cassandra Mills' output.

Only as they emerged from the blue-painted tunnel into the dusty cathedral of the factory did his synapses fire again. It was the noise rather than the heat that impressed him at first. He saw the familiar rigging of pulleys and masts, spindles and columns that would drag his fibre into a garment. The roof was gravid with tubing and insulation. Dotted around the room he saw the workers, pale blue shirts dark with sweat beneath their overalls. The variety of their colours and sizes shocked him – he'd expected the workers to be Negroes, wasn't that the way? – but there were whites too, plenty of them, blonde girls with blotchy arms and smudgy eyes, even a pair of Asiatic-looking twins. A red-haired man with sallow skin and bloodshot blue eyes leant on a trolley, taking breath from shifting crates. His hair crinkled back from a freckled scalp. He took in Alan along with a lungful of air.

Around the chamber, like pneumatic sunflowers, stood a few electric fans, rocking slightly with the effort. The silver metal of their blades was pitted with rust, drops of condensation fell about their stems. By Alan's calculation, fewer than a dozen of the fifty or so people in the room could feel any benefit from the breeze.

Over here, he heard Ray saying. Alan, over here. They walked down a ramp into a windowless area and there it was – a great cube of his yarn, yards and yards of twisted rope as thick as an arm, suspended on a square spindle. From the top a line fed on to a series of rollers; with each yard released, the square bale lurched in its cradle. Alan watched its apparent precariousness. He moved to the back of the structure and raised himself on to the balls of his feet to peer in and through the diamond-shaped gap, as if gazing from the rigging along the deck of a ship. Ray and the executives stood in contemplation halfway down the apparatus which stretched out maybe twenty-five yards. Through the fish-eye view, Alan saw his creation spin away from him out into the world.

In the boardroom they talked of certainties. Ratios and output, targets and results. A short history of the company, said the senior man. We moved here a couple of years ago from NY State. Alan heard the virtues of North Carolina, the nation's leading textile-manufacturing state. He nodded at the expertise, understood the stability of deals that kept decent working people and responsible management in partnership. People down here aren't fooled by smart-talking unions with their international agenda and holidays on the Black Sea. There's a tradition of benign employment here, of truly paternal management. Nobody wants to live through strikes again. A couple of years back there was some trouble and it all came down to union interference. But the governor himself, a man with considerable experience of the textile business, the governor intervened personally. And eventually it was resolved. One hell of an unpleasant business at the time, make no mistake. No one wants to see that kind of thing again. Especially now – with this uncertainty just a few hundred miles to the south. Alan gazed out of the window, past the insect screen, across down the parched grass to the tawny road. On the bend he saw a hoarding, white and red on blinding white, for No-Roach. No-Roach, he recalled from the morning paper. No need to move dishes and food in the kitchen, simply brush around or mix with liquid wax for floors. Cuba, Brazil and they guessed his people, Mr Hopkins, the British, well, they had Berlin. Countries without the benefit of democratic stability. Countries where communism could take hold almost overnight, like any pest, given the right conditions.

Alan imbibed so much certainty in that half-hour that he too was now unshakeable. Cassandra Mills were clearly first among equals. There would be no cause to look back. Mooncloud and Walden Brown and Spaceshot Graphite, even Mesa Verde, would run off the giant spindles into sparkling wash'n'wear careers. Over time, automation would reduce the hours those dejected people had to labour in the heat. They too would become more prosperous, less pressured, free to spend time on hobbies, perhaps with the opportunity to put together a little business of their own.

Ray was uncharacteristically quiet during the meeting. Far from asserting his northern know-how and presentational prowess, he appeared to demur to their hosts. In place of his typical indulgent superiority, the mill management were treated to an attentive pose, putting Alan in mind of the mongrel Tramp.

Ray's mood seemed to lift as they left the mill. He wound the windows down in the car, lit a cigarette and hummed: a mixed grill of Kenton, Ellington and Goodman. Alan was keener to talk. What was Ray's judgement on the mill? Did he think they were up to the task, to the volume and quality control? Yeah, sure, said Ray. I'm sure they could do it. And will do it? said Alan. Yeah, and maybe will do it.

Maybe?

Alan, said Ray. Just relax. Let's get back to the hotel – have a shower and a drink. I'll see you downstairs around five.

By five-thirty, Alan and Ray were seated on red leather benches at the corner of a square table at the Forest Grill, a restaurant perched on the edge of one of the city's many bowls and craters, all filled with towering vegetation. The roadside entrance to the Forest Grill was unassuming enough; but the grill room itself faced into a jungle of grey-green foliage, inches from the large plate-glass windows. Alan felt he might have difficulty breathing.

Three men arrived and sat on either side of Ray and Alan, pinning them closer to the green view. They introduced themselves by name, but not by organization. Beverages were ordered. After the joviality, a nervous silence fell.

"How much has Ray told you?" asked the oldest, a predatory type Alan was getting to recognize, well fed, grey but keen-eyed. Well, said Alan, looking sideways at Ray, almost apologizing for his own lack of understanding. He's said that you want to discuss the next stage for the fibre. So I suppose you gentlemen must be from licensing perhaps, or patents?

With some exchange of glances they agreed they did have patenting expertise between them, licensing also. There was another short silence, broken by a guffaw from Ray. Ray was grinning, too broadly. Well, Alan, as I was saying to you earlier, this is a delicate stage. These gentlemen would like to advise us on our options. Lawyers then? said Alan, smiling enquiringly at the group. Marketing? Distribution, surely not? Well, this is a diverting game.

Alan, these gentlemen are not from Lavenirre, said Ray. They're from another organization, a large one, I'm sure I need hardly spell out which one. They have a particular interest in the new fibre, a keen interest and they'd like to discuss with us ways it might best be deployed.

Alan rocked back on his bench, bouncing slightly against the stuffed back rest, breaking the pentagon of intent faces and clasped hands. Did these people look any different from his employers? Were they in fact emissaries sent to test his resolve? He glanced across at Ray, at his enlarged pupils, at the angle of his body towards the eldest man. The spiced smell of the hickory trees pressed down. Alan frowned at the framed photograph on the wall of the governor, with his wife in a strapless silk pyramid swinging out across the dance floor.

I have to admit, said the senior man, seeing Alan's circumspection, that we are a tad disappointed not to see this miraculous suit in action. Ray tells me you've been wearing it all day. How did it square up?

Fine, thank you, murmured Alan. Just fine. His neck still chafed from the knobbly edges of the collar. Mooncloud had an unexpectedly unyielding lining. He thought of its springiness when he'd removed the suit earlier back at the hotel.

(He'd been sweat-drenched and clumsy, fingertips tight with the heat, but the suit slid on to the bed in the same jaunty attitude as the previous evening. After he'd showered, he'd carried it carefully over his arm (he could concede now that it was rather sodden and soiled with dust from the mill) along the corridor, through the swing doors to the service stairs and on down to the basement. There he'd found the housekeeper dozing in her cubicle. She'd started at his approach – had she missed the call from reception? – but was reassured by his friendliness, then bemused by his request. Surely the suit should be sent out to the laundry, or maybe it just needed a little pressing. Very elegant, sir, she ventured, just the latest thing. Isn't it? he responded, delighted, holding it up for her to admire, kicking a little at the legs so they gambolled like Donald O'Connor. And now, he announced, prolonging the pantomime, and now . . . we are going to . . . wash it.

Wash it? She rolled her eyes. Oh dear me, no. No, sir. Not wash it. No.

Oh yes, he said. We need hot water. And soap flakes.

She stood, eyeing him doubtfully. You sure about this, sir? Her arms stayed firmly folded beneath her large bosom.

Yes, yes. The joke was expiring now; he wanted her to

witness the wonder of the next step. She scattered the waxy flakes into a wooden tub, whisking the suds with disapproval. Her dark arms descended into the steam, plunging the Mooncloud suit into the froth. It stiffened on contact with the water; and she raised her eyes at him in apprehension. Oh, my Lord.

Don't worry, he said. That's normal, be brutal with it; it's pretty strong – you can scrub it, even put it through the wringer. The housekeeper set about a small stain on the trouser knee. As she worked, she set up a rhythm. Three times to the right, twice to the left with a final flourish straight ahead. By the time she'd poured the water for the rinses, she was humming, even giggling at the ludicrous bulkiness of the suit, poking at it with wooden tongs.

They lifted it together, water splashing down into the tub. Mind yourself now, she warned. You shouldn't by rights be in here doing this. This is my work. Well, it's mine too, he said. How's that, she asked. He told her.

No, she kept saying. No, as they fed the jacket gently between the rollers of the mangle, set on its widest gauge. Who would think it? Just imagine, ten years from now, every room sending down each night a suit like this. Just imagine. Have to change the whole laundry. And I have seen the beginning, here. More than that, he told her, you have been part of the testing process, the true road testing of the product.

Imagine that, she had said. Shaking her head.)

And now the suit was hanging in the bath back at his

room, freeing itself of the last traces of damp. Ready for tomorrow. The suit was at the hotel, the formula was in his head and in a bunch of notes in the laboratory, the framework for its production all in place – except evidence of an alternative framework was now presenting itself. He considered the four men around him at the table. It was important not to shut off possibilities. Any experimental approach should be thorough, but flexible. What if . . .? What if the strength and tenacity he was seeking from the fabric was not matched by that of the company?

He needed to talk not just to Ray but to the most senior people in this rival empire. Obviously he'd been aware of them, as a shadow on his tail, but now they'd doubled ahead and were confronting him. In theory, this was simply an approach to be endured and rebuffed. His loyalty to Lavenirre was a given, a control. He couldn't be guilty of betrayal, it wasn't part of his character. In any case, he wouldn't welcome Farebrother as an opponent. But if you began from another premise, entirely, if it was no longer a question of loyalty to a distant management, but of loyalty to a concept, then you might end up with a different result. Depending on the criteria you employed, it might even be a better one.

Alan leant back into the ring of colleagues, a movement he would make hundreds, thousands, of times over the next decades. Businessmen. Together. In conference.

In the night, the crickets rasped in and out, up and down, like fingers on a grater.

At the hotel, Alan had to put his shoulder to the bathroom door where it came into conflict with the bumpy linoleum. He burst in to confront his pale startled face in the shaving mirror. For a moment, he was disorientated and fearful. Where was the suit? It was so simple; he'd been kept busy for the evening so the competition could snatch it away. But it was still there, partly obscured by the shower curtain, swinging gently on its hanger from the showerhead. He stepped forward and fingered the sleeve. No moisture. He felt the trouser cuffs; reassuringly dry. Colour and shape had held well. Good boy, good boy.

Methodically, he checked the seams and the pockets. He was going to need another shower himself. He hadn't been aware of it at the time, but since he'd been in the bathroom a miasma of exhausted body had hovered around him. He opened the new suit jacket wide to see if there were any anomalies showing in the lining, any signs of tension – and almost staggered back. The pert, bright weave of Mooncloud had shed the dirt and the moisture. The suit was bouncy and optimistic for the new day. It could be washed over and over like this and come up each time as fresh looking as the day the fibre first left the lab; but to his astonishment, an amazement mainly that he had not before made this connection, from this moment the suit could never shake off the one thing he hadn't counted on, a pungent and tenacious taint, disturbing and arousing, not modern, not convenient, not consumer-friendly, not wash'n'wear instant rebirth, but bound into the very fabric, the very fibre, permanently adherent. Stale sweat, the ineradicable smell of human experience.

12

ON SUNDAY morning at a quarter past nine the chimes zigzag from the black and cream speaker panel of the radio perched on the upstairs landing; a descending peal strikes out and tumbles over the edge, falling with Jimmy's lead E-type as it ricochets around the bend in the staircase and careers half-circle to a racing stop on the hall parquet. "Arse about face" mutters the proxy driver admiringly from the landing, out of his mother's earshot.

Over and over, the bells from this morning's place of worship stun and clang on the Home Service, summoning Sunday: there are those who will still be drawn out to a real church, although for many the broadcast service will be along in a minute. When they will worship, privately, "in their own way". The Hopkins belong to a third set, the increasing number for whom Sunday ritual is leisurely cooked breakfast and cleaning the car - preparation for the communion of riding lessons or lunch with relatives or simply the inevitable, inexorable post-prandial drive.

Sausage and bacon and ketchup. The fat and ketchup run into furrows made by the fork, adding another layer of twirls and explosions to the pattern at the centre of the plates. Jimmy chases his around with fried bread. Then he gets on his bike and cycles vertiginously to the newsagent on the green, leaning low over the handlebars, dipping into the bends, daring the chocolatey track to reach up and claim him as he skids up the old ditch by the pond. Faster yet. If he pedals until his muscles groan, the wind in his ears could be the roar of Hailwood on the TT course.

He buckles the papers into the canvas roll bag behind the saddle and heads home, but this time he's riding back to Laramie with supplies for the homestead and the pace is easier, although his horse bucks a little from time to time. Those rattlesnakes are darned crafty, disguising themselves as tree roots.

At home he desperately wants to look at the sports pages, but the papers, he knows, are for Donald and Evie. When they've finished, then he may look, if they say so. No one likes to have their paper all crumpled before they read it. But then Patsy relents (a development he cannot quite fathom) so he carefully opens the *Sunday Express* from the back, placing that day's front page bride face down on the table, her newsprint tulle and organza pressed against the matrix pattern on the Formica.

From half past nine to a quarter to twelve very little

happens. Lucy and Sally squabble over a doll's blanket. Patsy plaits Lucy's hair, humming to herself, tugging sharply at the stray strands. Lucy whimpers as the red ribbon binds around the pigtails. Then they march in flannel shorts and checked dresses in the high sun across the road, catching in the corners of their eyes the vestigial movements of the close – the flicker of a figure behind a bevelled glass door, the swish of a hedge-clipper. In the hush of Evie and Donald's hall, a grandfather clock ticks through the polish-scented air.

The French windows are open to the terrace. Jimmy sits in the velour armchair, one knee knocking against the side. He exaggerates the movement, daring Patsy's reprimand, but she has installed herself on the step, her arms clasped around her knees, face upturned to the sun, eyes closed. His mother looks a little strange, and he's not sure she should be sitting on the floor like that in somebody else's house. Donald is having a serious discussion with Sally over a dish of potato crisps. From the kitchen, he can hear Evie pouring liquids and stacking plates, a soundtrack punctuated by the occasional metallic clash. Why isn't Mum in there with her, helping, like she usually does?

Donald has opened the newspaper and Jimmy tries to read the back page again, surreptitiously, because it would be bad manners otherwise and Patsy might see him from her vantage point on the step. Within a few moments, however, Donald has dropped the paper low enough to fix Jimmy with his bi-focals. Oh-oh, now he's for it. But

Donald wants his opinion. Should the BBC have decided to end the Sports Special transmission of Football League matches? The Corporation reckons there's not sufficient interest; from now on they'll broadcast games on a purely *ad hoc* basis, if they're of particular significance. Jimmy nods sagely, speed sports are the thing now – motor racing and motorcycles – in his opinion. Horse racing too. It's hard to get so involved in soccer on the television screen. Everyone's too small.

Donald passes on to the news section of the *Sunday Times* and hands the *Express* to Patsy.

She reads out to them, in what Jimmy thinks is a funny voice, too fast, embarrassing. Her real voice is lower. He'd be told off if he read like that. British troops in the Middle East are restraining Iraq from attacking Kuwait. It will all be over soon so long as the Russkies don't get involved, adds Donald. Beyond the headlines, fashion is in a marshmallow mood. This is the summer of bare arms, of hair a little longer and gently waved, of matt slub-surfaced rayon available in sugar-pink, green and sand, while in the kitchen it's cucumber with mushroom and prawns. Lucy sits beside Patsy at the threshold of the French doors and together they speculate on the ranking for the newspaper's £1,000 Gala Dress contest. They sort the contenders for elegance and "general appearance"; for fitting in, not looking out of place. *Comme il faut*, articulates Evie from the doorway, with a knowing nod to Sally.

The children sip squash from precarious glasses, engraved with fleur-de-lys. Their fingers clutch at the stems. Donald's long digits form comfortable angles around a tumbler of gin and tonic as in turn he reads aloud. On television some "egghead" has suggested the desirability of finding an alternative drug to alcohol. Laughter from the adults. And Louis Jourdain (cheers from Evie) has pipped the Duke of Edinburgh as the world's handsomest man. Well, it's evident, she boasts, flourishing a tea towel triumphantly.

Matters of economics and finance are there too, but on a Sunday, with the children there and the sun shining, they don't bother about those. Donald puts the pages aside for later in the evening, with a little cold ham, hemi-spheres of tomato, mustard and a small pyramid of salt. Cold collation, darling. It makes Evie shudder, so flat, so British, but Donald teases that it's his favourite meal of the week.

It's all very perplexing anyway: on the one hand, the country is clearly gleaming with progress, the advertise-ments trumpet the showpiece steel works at Ravenscraig and Consett, cutting at the gleaming edge. Half a million pounds spent every twenty-two hours, Jimmy does the mental calculation under Donald's tutelage, would that be nearly four million pounds a week? Donald doesn't believe in nearly, and traces the digits of the final annual investment on a sheet of paper with one of the 2H pencils to hand on his reading table. One hundred and ninety-nine million, ninety thousand seven hundred and ten pounds, if you discount the fraction. Which Jimmy certainly does. Oh dear, Patsy holds her hands up in mock helplessness. Aren't you both clever? It's all way beyond me.

Her gesture has the desired effect. It deflects attention from the cavalcade that runs in her head. She sits in the doorway, with her bare arms wrapped again across her midriff, the pale fabric of her dress ruched into folds that cut as deep as the drag in her pelvis, the thirst in her bones. While Jimmy runs through his nine-times table for Donald, she turns to look out at the lawn, edged with miniature white posts, little white ropes hanging between them. She sees instead Jon walking towards her in some restaurant, perhaps abroad. The place is full, but with people who do not know her, or him. So when he reaches down to greet her, placing one hand suavely on her shoulder, she slips her arms around his neck and, imperceptibly, her tongue between his teeth. As Holly Golightly does.

After lunch, Donald proposes a drive, but before that he produces his cine-camera and the children cavort in the garden for posterity. They rush towards the lens and mug and mime, eager auditioners in the role of unknown child for when the film is exhumed from the attic long after Donald's death. Cine-film makes Patsy nervous, she flutters her eyelashes at the camera and twists on her heel; her bony wrists flap Donald away. It makes her sad too. A flicker of the shutter and years of judgement.

The children will need cardigans for the drive. They will, really, Patsy insists and as they tumble in turn to spend pennies in the pink and green downstairs cloak-room, with its regiment of Edwardian silhouettes, she sets off through the hush of the entrance hall. I'll leave the door on the latch, she calls, although no one is listening. The Drive feels warm through her shoe leather; her toes, reaching beyond the sole, catch occasionally on the loose gravel. The long key to the front door is cool in her hand and she shudders slightly at the empty house in front of her, thrilled at the prospect of being there unaccompanied. That Hide and Seek feeling again.

By the front door, she is in shadow and she shivers, this time from the drop in temperature, willing her fingers to manipulate the key into the awkward lock. It yields as she pushes, forcing a sigh from the draft excluder around the door frame.

Inside, the outlines of the rooms are distorted by the gloom. The cat comes chirruping through from the kitchen.

On the mat is a rectangle. The envelope is blue-grey. Nausea touches her: it is addressed to her but she does not recognize the careful writing. Although she guesses.

She picks it up carefully, trying to read the meaning from its appearance. She turns it over; the flap is sealed down evenly. She places a fingernail in the crease and tugs it open gently. There is only one sheet inside.

Closing the door behind her, she walks into the kitchen and over to the window. The warm light bounces off the sink, casting luminous bars on to her dress and the paper in her shaking hands. At the top of the sheet is a thread of gum, like a hangnail, where the page has been torn from the pad.

There are only two paragraphs and one of those is barely a sentence long. He is so very sorry, she is the most beautiful woman he has ever met and she deserves to be happy, he really hopes she will be and that everything will work out for the best, he will never ever forget her. His signature is neat and constrained, the J barely larger than the N. There is a small crisscross flourish beneath, a demure tail folding itself under.

She drags her eyes up to the first paragraph, but the words refuse to remain in order. She registers difficult and hard and stop and please and wish and different and a short line that sticks out and cannot be ignored. I owe her everything, you see. I would die rather than hurt her. And wrong, the word wrong, there near the top and again at the end of the paragraph. Twice wrong.

Patsy frowns and tries again to make sense of the lines. She strains to hear his voice, but these words are not his voice, not the gentle, teasing voice that she can summon up when she lies in bed at night, her hand resting between her thighs. This is a tight tone, with more sorrow than anger, embarrassed, reproving in its twisting regret. So she returns to the second paragraph and bathes, briefly, in the tempting solace of his future memories of her never to be forgotten beauty.

When the anger comes, it hits her so hard she has to grip the hot metal of the sink. What is wrong? She is wrong. If there is wrong, then it cannot come from him; he is the one who has identified it. It must be her. How could he, who stood in this kitchen, holding her gaze (then her body) too long, how dare he find now that it was wrong, something to be pushed away? He, who hasn't the education or style to write a proper letter, or even tear a sheet of cheap writing paper clean off the pad? Galvanized, she wants to rend and scream. She wants to frighten him and hurt him and have him rush headlong to console her, to bend her ferocity back into the abandon it is howling to be.

She grasps the damp dishcloth and twists until the water bleeds into the sink. Then she turns and sinks to her haunches on the chequered floor, her back against the green kitchen unit. The cat picks its way across the glossy black squares and weaves an S in front of her shins. She can feel its fur through the nylons. Her ankles, wobbling on the slingbacks, begin to ache but the sob is still rising and she waits, one hand caressing the cat's head, for it to tear out.

The knife is too large and inexact; glass would be sharper, more devastating. A fall might be clumsy. She wants fire and sufficient pain to lose consciousness. And she wants to leave no trace. Then she sees the children picking through the ashes (of what? The house? Her body?) and sees there is no end to the mess.

At least she didn't forget the cardigans. She has a run in her stockings where the cat attempted to climb on her lap, the cool flannel has failed entirely to reduce the inflammation around her neck and eyes and she's kept everyone waiting for twenty minutes. So sorry, couldn't find a thing, everything all packed away. And would you believe, the cat had been sick in the kitchen.

It wasn't, protests Jimmy, looking at her curiously. It wasn't packed away, it was on the back of the chair in my room. And Lucy's was folded on her bed, like normal.

Shush now, I realize that now, clever-clogs, she laughs. Easy enough now – but honestly, you wouldn't credit the mess over there, Evie. I just don't know where I am.

Evie, who has donned her white summer blazer, has been sitting on the hall chair with her neat ankles crossed.

"Yes, yes, but the children have been waiting and waiting, and I don't know now if we have time to take them," and she mentions the name of a local expanse of heathland where the adults can observe from a bench while the children play Indians in the sand and heather, finding "arrowheads" among the bulbous stones.

"I am sorry. I'm so sorry, but I expect there would still be time – wouldn't there, Donald?" Patsy appeals to him without looking directly, keeping her swollen eyes safely downcast, even behind her sunglasses.

"Oh yes, of course, darling," he responds, pulling on his driving gloves, easing the webbing over his long fingers. "Take no notice of the Gorgon. She's too excited at the prospect of going out."

Patsy catches the tiny flicker of amusement in Evie's glance and feels a pit of loss open up beneath her. "Would you mind awfully, with the packing and all this mess still to clear up, if I didn't come along this time? I'm sure the children would behave themselves – and," she hears her voice rising, searching, "and there would be more room in the back without me, anyway."

"Mummy," whispers Lucy urgently, "Mummy, can I stay with you?" The plaintive final syllable stretches out.

"Nonsense, whatever for?" Patsy shakes her off. She sees Evie's head incline. "You'll have a wonderful time, darling, you know you love it there. Off you go now."

They go. The Rover proceeds out of the Close like a pregnant slug launching into a rumba.

The "click" of the look has passed by. The jaunty mismatch of coloured cups and saucers is no longer bohemian but amateur; the scarlet with the sky-blue in particular puts her teeth on edge. Cloudy water stains streak the metal knives and forks in the sink drainer. The turquoise design on the oatmeal jug looks more dirty than hand-painted. In the living room, the fission of the "Atomic" carpet is compromised by fragments of paper and string that the carpet sweeper refuses to swallow. In the playroom, "Sunburst" is eclipsed by packing cases while, upstairs in the children's room, "Boomerang" flings yellow and aubergine missiles on to a terracotta background but their progress is impeded by pieces of green Plasticine. All the little touches – the old glass shade tucked into a brass jardinière for a most individual lamp, the hand-painted colouring on the acrylic pendant or the coffee percolator with its double bowls and connecting pipes – seem off kilter and dusty.

No one who walked in now would see anything but the ugly truth. The breezy Mediterranean sensuality has gone, taking with it originality and charm, above all charm. The trompe l'oeil view into a hazy valley is a magazine picture glued behind a splintering piece of trellis.

And the lounge; she can hardly bear to look at the lounge. The metal trim around the new fireplace has already started to twist away from the wall. Without a fire, it looks like a food cabinet, or a display case from the pharmacists. Jimmy helped her make a proper blaze a couple of nights ago. They piled in old cardboard boxes and a broken balsawood dinosaur whose vertebrae cracked and curled in the flames. Jimmy enthused obligingly but she could see the placing was all wrong. The light from the fire fell only a few inches from the recess and you had to perch in the corner on the end of the sofa to catch it at all. Thank God Alan won't see it, at least for a year or so. What was she thinking of? She tried for a bold gesture and she's been left with an ugly scar. In any case, Alan would never have understood the romance of naked flames, would he? She can't remember any more what he likes, what excites him apart from formulae and laboratory trials, but even as she thinks this she knows it isn't fair, and the unfairness of it makes her want to weep. Alan can be enthusiastic, just not about her, not these days, or that's the way it seems to her. Perhaps she can't find the time or the space or the courage to be generous to him. Intimacy is so much easier with someone you're just getting to know.

She cannot believe there will be another place to make anew, to remodel, to start afresh. And even if there were, she no longer has the talent for it. Rolled up in the corner, the old shaggy rug looks yellowed. Even if she hauled all the furniture back into place, it wouldn't fit any more. The moment has passed.

She went further, impossibly further, than she should have done, but that's not the worst of it. What devastates her now is the knowledge that she would have done more. She would have dragged Jon on and down. She is stranded now, fully measuring the breadth of her contravention, but not yet plumbing its depth. What might she have been capable of if he had not cut her off like this? She is horrified, but cheated, too.

Would she have padded after him, like the red-eyed white cat across the way, always pregnant to some tom, teats stretching down to the pavement? An embarrassment to the street. Some joke now: in his leatherette suite Rookin will be laughing out of the side of his mouth. Oh dear, Mrs Hopkins, bit of a mess, eh? Dear, oh dear. Theatre in the round, I suppose. *Cinéma vérité*?

13

*H*EY KIDS *(look how easy it is to be American . . .),*
This could be the last letter before I see you all.

They're gradually getting used to me at the company. I'm
obviously not as good as the home-grown product, in their
opinion, but the problem is we're very good at learning in Britain,
probably the best. So keep at the sums.

The house is nearly ready — some of the cases have arrived
already. How funny our things look here. Yes, there is a pool and
a big terrace at the back where we can put up a telescope, Jimmy,
and watch all that activity up there. Perhaps we could launch our
own rocket one day. The garden, well, let's say there's plenty of
scope. It's grass, really, what they call a yard and it just stretches
into trees, no garden fence, no neighbours on top of you. Plenty
of space.

Since I last wrote I've been down South, and now I'm
headed even further down, almost Mexico way, to Florida.
Alligators, kids, snapping at my heels, like Peter Pan. Tell

Mummy I've not been able to phone, very busy indeed.
  Big hugs,

  Daddy

From the windows of the Flamingo Ridge Country Club, the links stretched down to the water. Alan could see the blue-white arcs of the tall lights on the jetty, outshining the moon. Little figures picked their way across, negotiating their way in or out of motor launches.

Inside the ballroom the light was electric yellow. Flickering candle bulbs in the grand chandeliers cast lines on the features of the members of the Synthetic Fibre Association of America, and their spouses, gathered for the summer convention. Alan had arrived for dinner with Ray and Marian. She wore pink wild silk empire line, her hair augmented with a coiled topknot. I may not enjoy the services of Alexandre de Paris, she told Alan when he complimented her, but I can still turn out my own little show. Let me introduce myself, said Ray. I am the man who accompanied Marian Daniels to Miami.

At dinner, on Marian's advice to be adventurous, Alan had mistakenly ordered Seafood Nantua. Ray, along with the herd, stuck to Beef à la Mode. Then Alan was driven with the rest of the crowd into the ballroom for an annual ritual – you won't believe this, Alan, these guys go ape - a revue of contemporary developments in the industry, a musical burlesque performed by textile executives on a stage erected at one end of the gilded hall. Alan sat beside Marian in a twilight Nina Ricci haze; the chandeliers had been dimmed, thank God. Ray was to his left, pivoting to catch this eye or shake that hand. As the pianist vamped the overture – Porter, Berlin, a little rock'n'roll – Ray hailed acquaintances, ducking along the row to squeeze a shoulder or punch a rib. He's inexhaustible, isn't he? said Alan. Marian turned her sleepy eyes on him. Uh-huh, she said, except when it comes to cleaning the pool. When is it now that your wife and children arrive, Alan? We are so looking forward to meeting them.

And they you, said Alan. I am sure you and Patsy will get along splendidly, he said without conviction. Tell me, Marian, what exactly is going to happen here, what do they do? Oh honey, I don't precisely know, but the tunes are good and the singing is real professional – it's something of a tradition now. Just try to enjoy what you can.

At the fringes of the stage, there was a frenzy of business. Huge cue cards were stacked in a clearing near the front of the audience. Mysterious bulges and ripples disturbed the makeshift curtain. The lights dropped right down and a cavalcade of sketches on the follies and foibles of the industry paraded before an audience entertained and bemused in equal measure. The men roared at the topical references, growling at the odd political jibe, at loose threads and threats and reds, at a young president who'd made a dodgy call (and the more they growl, the more we tremble, thought Alan, remembering Patsy's periodic 3am contemplation of the children's effort to survive in an atomized desert); the women smiled indul-gently at the costumes and ignored the strong language and the politics. Pirates and cavemen, cowboys and Roman centurions, a Pierrot and a Chaplin and an Ed Sullivan, Hawaiian maidens and harem girls manoeuvred their way on to the tiny stage and delivered their pitch square on to their audience. It's a great British tradition too, said Alan to Marian, men dressing up as women. He turned to look at Ray, but found the seat empty again. He glimpsed him shortly after, crouching at the end of one of the front rows.

What seemed like seconds later, Ray was back. Meet me by the rear door in ten, he whispered to the side of Alan's neck. Alan raised a hand in helpless protest – well, I don't know . . .? – but Ray had disappeared into the increasingly dishevelled crowd as men craned or stood to watch their colleagues and competitors belt out "South of the Border" with specific topical reference to Corduronne or Fibrolyne, or "I Love You, Darlonyl" complete with Maurice Chevalier boater and large man with hairy legs in French maid outfit, called Fluflette, which Alan could only suppose was some kind of Nylon blend. Alan closed his eyes for an instant, lost in the energetic incomprehensibility of it. There was nothing he could do, except exchange sultry smiles with Marian, maybe place a protective arm around the back of her chair when the large enthusiast behind her rose to his feet. And why not, in a few more minutes, make his excuses and join Ray for some further exploratory conversation? It was only a series of words, little more than those endless open-ended skirmishes with Ray's wife, conversations that became daily more intimate, without, it seemed to him, any greater urgency. They weren't, were they, leading to the position which she might think he'd made a pass? He couldn't imagine that kind of awkwardness in so laconic, and somehow distant, a relationship. Anyway, there was nothing he could do about it and frankly, he wasn't sure Ray would give a damn. Ray was motoring on something else.

Patsy, on the other hand, would make Marian look blowsy, and intentionally. She'd be brighter and sharper, with clearer features. Too much makeup, she'd sniff, the skill lies in making it look invisible. Honestly. And she'd be right, of course, but Alan doesn't know, he can feel more than a little stolen away by Marian's excess.

Onstage the Lost Sales Boys were squabbling over seats in Neverland. Alan recognized the technique. Ray had told him how, in high sales periods, it was standard procedure to remove one or two desks from the office, make it more uncomfortable for the boys to rest back at base. Crude but effective. He laughed along.

Would you, he murmured to Marian as an oversized Tiger Lily admonished a tiny, pot-bellied Peter Pan, excuse me for a minute? She winked her consent and he apologized his way to the end of the row.

It wasn't much cooler out on the terrace, but there was a breeze. He saw the congregation of glowing cigarette ends by the arbour. Alan, said Ray, all this covert activity, we apologize; it's just that the guys will need a decision by Monday at the very latest. I think you've had enough time.

Alan, said the senior man from the rival company. I've nothing new to say. You know the offer – complete control over research, a chance to be a pioneer in a research park where IBM and GE have already committed, no union problems and for you and your family a very attractive state to live in – clean air, good country, as many crab derbies and beach barbecues as you want within an hour or two's drive . . . there's no point in repeating it again. Ray? Let's get an answer on this tomorrow, shall we?

Will do, sir.

Don't worry about Marian, says Ray. I've asked that young Italian from marketing to make sure she gets back to the hotel. You and I, however, have a little trip to make.

Ray calls a cab and Alan falls dutifully into it. The cab swings around the drive, past the water plume in the lake, skirting the seventh and nine holes. Where are we going? asks Alan. Ray is humming and doesn't answer. He continues to beat on the armrest in the middle of the seat, grinning and grimacing along with the rhythm, holding Alan's gaze. Is this more quiet persuasion, says Alan, another group of people telling me I'll be doing the right thing by the fibre if I kidnap it and take it away from

Lavenirre? Ray shakes his head slowly, in time. No, Alan, you know that already. This, pal, is just you and me out together, on the town, on this beautiful hot night. Planning our future.

Alan sighs and sinks back in his seat. He has to say the unsayable. Ray, what if I didn't go, if we just stayed put?

Man, says Ray, you can't stay still. You've got to keep moving, ahead of the rest. This is a good deal. It makes you someone, more than just someone promising. And besides, if you stay, these guys are on to you already. You think someone in that little North Carolina mill isn't going to find he's taken some old rag home by mistake, rolled up in his dirty overalls? And – my, my – isn't this rag a piece of that strange new stuff they're working on in the end mill-room, the one that's out of bounds for everyone except "authorized personnel"? Well, goodness, he did just hear that someone might be interested in that.

And *do* they already have a piece of the test fabric? asks Alan, suddenly cool.

Couldn't say for sure, but my suspicion is they do. Ray has stopped drumming on the armrest now and is gazing out of the window at the hotels sailing past.

Oh, I see, says Alan, and relaxes into a familiar process of recognition. There is this new piece of information that Ray has just thrown into his lap, but there is also another shape behind it somewhere that he is starting to identify. Just wait, he thinks, just wait and it will all fall into place.

Ever since he was a little boy, Alan has been good at puzzles. The twists of interlocking metal that arrived in

crackers were always despatched by him before the last
coloured paper hat had been squeezed on to a relative's
head. He never found books of optical illusions much fun
either, because the alternative images were equally
apparent to him on first viewing. This castle is also a
grinning crone, this foreground is that background, a
woman is also a cat. What really intrigues Alan is not
ambiguity but finding patterns and balancing equations,
because these solutions often lead to new discoveries. He
needs time to let his thoughts percolate through the layers
of acquired knowledge. It's hard to find that time at
home. Here it's easier, when Ray stops talking.

At the entrance, they dip out from the cab and are sub-
sumed at once into a new colony of tuxedoed ants. Lines
stream up the pale steps, knots of individuals elongate
into chains, exchanging cigarettes and greetings. Now
this *is* a business, says Ray, steering Alan by the elbow
through the throng. This really is a business. *Look* at all
these people.

In the foyer Ray is greeted by a young man who presses
tickets into his hand. Ray dispenses in return a handshake
backed up by the left hand to the elbow – brief, warm,
conclusive. They are now authorized personnel. From the
wall of beaten brass doors that give on to the great
auditorium comes the metallic sound of drum brushes
teasing through the vibraphone. Louder than the music,
though, is the buzz of men at work, engaged in fraternal

barter and badinage. They impress and compete, affirming and undermining between the tumblers and ashtrays. Alan reads the banners festooned over the doorways. Annual Disc Jockeys' Convention. Miami, Florida.

Ray takes them down the carpeted stairs to their table in the second tier, raked up against the stage of the great bowl. Down there the roar is louder; the other occupants of the table shout across at one another, lit from beneath by the tiny brazier in the centre of the white linen circle. The trio onstage struggle against the fractional delay of the PA system, the rolling voice of the crowd and the chink of china and glass; the bass player is lost anyway, away in his own world. They finish their number and leave the stage to isolated outbreaks of applause.

As the next band negotiates its boxes and cylinders on to the apron, Ray turns away from his neighbour to introduce Alan. Brilliant scientist, announces Ray, wonderful discovery. You wait; it will transform lives. You just wait. Alan murmurs his embarrassment. Not that you'd know it from him, continues Ray. He's the guy they had in mind for that gin advert – you've seen it? – "No wonder the British have kept cool for a hundred and ninety-two years." The other man smiles and nods and dives in to intercept an exchange on the other side of the table about another innovation that really will shake up people's lives.

Come on, Alan, says Ray, just commit. You know you will. It's pretty much the only option. Without us, they'll go ahead with a generic in no time. But with you, they can be market leader. It's the only option. Hey, here she is.

And on to the stage in a misty spotlight undulates the singer, the disc jockeys' darling, that famous black voice in a white body. She *is* white, too, Alan notes, powdered creamy platinum, with only the hint of flesh beneath. She's young, maybe still in her twenties, but stately. Her shoulders are soft, like dusted marzipan. Her dress is another white again, pearly, like teeth, or bones, stiff, gleaming fabric, some kind of treated cotton, he guesses, with a metallic satin sheen, wrapped tight around her torso and shooting out full to the floor. Her hair is bleached to ivory, folded into a gauzy French pleat. The spotlight shimmers around her.

The audience whoop and applaud, cigarettes clenched between their teeth, as she stands before the microphone. Her speaking voice is heavy and slow, but slightly disjointed, as though words are only available to her in groups of two or three. She introduces the celebrated pianist and his quintet, barely moving her head in their direction. Then she sweeps her eyes, teasing or myopic, over the chattering dark. Shall we, she intones, swing a little? And the house erupts as the piano player launches into his famous time signature; the singer smiles towards him, laying a curved arm along the frame of the Steinway, breathes deep into that bloomy body and turns to the microphone, dropping her phrases easily over the band's complex architecture. In the dark, men turn to each other and shake their heads with pleasure. Isn't she just . . .?

Alan bathes in the reflected stardust. She is indeed. She's the sugar plum fairy and the fairy godmother too, dispensing dreams. The voice is sensuous and knowing, an older voice, bluesy but not threatening. She's been in those hotel rooms, left behind when the out-of-towner returns to his wife, but she'll sigh and pay the bill, not scramble out of the bathroom window. Alan admires the frankness of the wry confession: love's no more than a curtain-raiser to pain. This thought is exciting, reckless. He loves this directness in American women. He loves the way they look at him; how they are curious but not demanding, how they show their enthusiasms, almost like children; how they're not afraid to dislike. It's relaxing and exciting to be around them. For the first time in his life, he finds that women seek out his company at social occasions. They talk to him about his interests. They want to know. He, in turn, feels he can ask them almost intimate questions about themselves and by happy chance these questions appear to unleash a stream of goodwill. Maybe, one day, when he's not in the lab or at a meeting, he'll be able to talk to women for much of the time. Women like this. Maybe, one day, he'll be able to talk to his own wife a little more like this – the day she turns from a problem he tries to solve into one side of a perfect equation.

Conversation in the concert bowl has begun to rise again, bridging the singer's phrases. How can they, thinks Alan, cradling another scotch, when she's the star, up there against the purple-black firmament, and they adore her? How can they talk over her voice like that? He looks at his own table where Ray is locked once more in debate with his neighbour. They are discussing airtime and advertising, reach and markets. Potential. The radio man wants to know about consumer trends. More than three hundred thousand factory workers will lose their jobs through automation over the next year. But there's opportunity, he states, as if discovering gravity, there's opportunity here. If home-makers loosen the purse strings, it could put the economy back on track. The ladies may well be a force in the land. Ray acts as if this news is a revelation to him too. Alan frowns at their footwork: he still hasn't quite mastered the business square dance. But he will. Within a few minutes, each of the two men is repeating back to the other his own argument, without any obvious self-consciousness. A perfect balance.

Behind them the singer closes her eyes and laments the man who was stolen away, the life spun out alone. Listen to her, urges Alan silently, she's gorgeous, even if she's not entirely authentic – who could really steal from this luscious creature? Even as her performance moves him, his mind is starting to engage elsewhere as it often does, tangling with the notion of perpetual performance he read about in one of the faded papers in Ray's den. He tries to imagine it: this, repeated over and over again, in some digital format he can't yet fathom, in a thousand places each night, could it evoke the same emotion? The audience, of course, would be different each time, often more attentive than this herd of diners, lone listeners sat plumb in the middle of the settee, at the perfect apex for the stereo sound, in the perfect seat to watch the soft-focus shoulders rise and fall for the high notes. Not always, though, the disc (if it were a disc) would spin on other occasions to an empty room, or one full of revellers, or be the soundtrack for a couple making love. Or is this performance the only real one?

The singer is taking a break now (strange how someone so assured and relaxed when singing freezes over the spoken word) and Alan looks wistfully at the tail of her spotlight as it sails off the stage. Perhaps this can be the only true performance. From now on, any replaying has lost the key element, suspense. He can't be entirely sure that she will ever come back out, that she won't collapse in the second half or pick a fight with the Cuban exile percussionist (feelings are still running high, after all, national pride is badly stung) or that a cry of "Jezebel" might ring, incongruously from the dark depths as she lingers over "Salt Lake City Blues". And without this potential it's already dead. Once recorded, it will have to be presented in its best light, edited in some way, cleaned up, made history. It's a process he's already familiar with: in fact, at two o'clock this morning, he was sitting at the wooden table by the window in his hotel room, drafting an abstract for a new variation of fibre, positing an extra chain to reduce the odour adherence. Alanylene (thank God, thank God, it never came to that) may prove no more than a diversion, a cul-de-sac in the development of the next generation of synthetic fibres. Or that's the way he's already started to write it up.

Ray, of course, doesn't know this. Ray is still playing in the live version, where eloping with the new fibre will make him richer and more desirable than he is already. Ray did enquire whether he would be wearing the suit again and Alan replied, a little snappy for him, that today he did not feel like playing a walking doll. Alan wonders how long it will be before the competition makes the same simple discovery he did. Perhaps they'll assume that all those practical tests have been carried out. In that case, it's hardly his place to put them right. His place, from now on, is in the bosom of Lavenirre. This evening, after he'd struggled into what he's learnt to call a tux, he made that telephone call to Farebrother at home, warning of (not confessing to, he's also learning fast about presentation) the weakness among the fibre's properties, that weakness that makes it, well, virtually unwearable, to be frank. Then he revealed Ray's intention to defect.

For a nervous moment, he heard nothing from the other end of the line. Alan has by now no need of Farebrother's physical presence to sense his potential for violence. Then came a wheeze and the chuckle. Alan could imagine a little shine breaking out on the head. "Well, Hopkins, this situation is not without its entertainment. Let's let him go, with the damned stuff," and gruffly, "fuck him."

Thank God, thought Alan, for that sheaf of new ideas he'd delivered to Farebrother's desk a fortnight before. He hadn't thought it an insurance policy, at the time. But it will serve him well.

For now, though, he leans back into Ray's yearning charm. Alan is beginning to realize how susceptible he is to charm. He's not had that much experience of it up until now, but he already has an inkling that it's possible to partake of it without commitment. Charm was frowned on at home as an indicator of dishonesty. Criminals had charm. Succumbing to charm meant a deposit lost or a heart broken. People didn't get to positions of worth through charm. Patsy has a careful charm, of course, which impressed him in their first meetings, but it's chiefly of a practical kind. Mostly, she uses it to get things done; she doesn't splash it around. He sometimes wishes she had some to spare. Over the years from now, Alan will learn to enjoy people in a recreational way, be amused by them, be amusing to them, without taking his eyes far from the one true cause, the Corporation. Patsy, one day, with the wisdom of a brief spell of therapy, will cite Alan's fear of intimacy and concede, grudgingly, that his second wife (company psychologist, that's a joke) seems to have conquered this fear, and with considerable zeal. In fact, Patsy might welcome a little more reticence these days – what's the point in going over it all again? It's dead and buried, why does he always have to identify causes? Her therapist will frown at the heresy.

His colleagues will attribute Alan's courteous ruthlessness to his British reserve; they'll rarely see his hands move, and never catch him with blood on them: no one really gets to know him, they'll remark among themselves. As he will do about them at intervals when he returns to the Home Counties. Oh, Americans are very hospitable, he will say, almost reflexive in their hospitality. And first names, of course, and really remarkably informal in business. But it's a distant land with strange customs. Don't fool yourself.

This night, in the smoky, starry bowl, he's not entirely fooled about himself. Later, he'll have devised his own business code – a system he can refer to when advising younger colleagues, a catalogue of his decisions that passes for an ethical career. Tonight, though, he is repeating to himself the "lesser of two evils" argument. Ray, this man across the table, his guide and companion for the past four and a half weeks, has recently taken on the aspect of the Eden snake. Alan has no choice; he must be loyal to the Corporation that brought him over here. It's a secondary issue that only he (and now one other) knows that the wonder fabric has lost its lustre, gained a miasma and become a liability, that he's not at this very moment the catch that the opposition thinks he is. In any case, maybe Ray has really become no more than a phase he's out-grown. For a time there, he was quite under Ray's spell. Everything about the man was contagious, easy, even admirable. But already that seems a long time ago.

So, before he picks up his glass and clinks it against Ray's, Alan makes a briefly surprising finding for a man schooled in decency and fair play. He can live with letting Ray hang out to dry. This discovery could be devastating to his view of himself, but from now on he simply won't have time for that.

Alan is tumbling like an astronaut in his capsule, withdrawing into himself, starting the slow spin as he begins re-entry to the atmosphere.

14

THE THIRTY-THREE bus will be along in a minute. Any moment the bulging elder trees on the bend will lurch as it swings into view with a hydraulic hiss. Patsy sits back in the wooden shelter; through a missing knot in the panelling she keeps one eye on the curving road. Her stomach muscles contract. It's a trial, she'll let them relax at the first glimpse of the green and yellow vehicle. She holds her bag on her knee; the two orbs on the gilt clasp press past each other between her fingers.

She is dressed for shopping, or the dentist, in a responsible two-piece. Her wrists flex inwards, displaying the watch face or shaking the charms on the bracelet. She knows exactly where she is going – once, almost apologetically, he pointed it out to her as they drove past – but she has no idea what she will do when she gets there.

The day is overcast but warm. The sweat lies cool in her armpits and in the creases of her groin; her fingers are cold and dry and shaking. It is Tuesday, which she may or may not remember as being a day off. I have to get back on time tonight, he may have said: Tuesday's her day off. Or Thursday. Recalled conversations seem unlikely now, unreliable: she's worn them out. Sometimes she finds herself reordering, even rewriting, them, inserting life or death claims or romantic, open-ended observations. But now it is Tuesday, a day that seems open and ugly, dangerous.

The town is proceeding with its business as she lurches above it. In the High Street, market stalls are starting to dismantle. Under violet helmets, shampooed hair begins to set. Through café windows couples stare past each other at the oncoming pedestrians, while quadrants of meat pie steam in front of them. And four foot up, Patsy begins to consider alighting at the next stop, pulling the cord to alert the driver that she has thought again.

The greasy flock of the seat digs through the Tricel into her thighs. Perhaps if he glimpses her across the street, he'll realize. He'll realize that passion is unstoppable. Then they can escape together to some coastal inn or rural hotel and . . . and she can be free . . . to . . . be so much more than she is. So much more than Alan could ever guess.

Instead she rattles around in a void, sometimes glad it's all over and normal service can be resumed, sometimes desperate to recapture that new-minted feeling – the most sparkling she's ever been, with the least expectation that she would sparkle. But like thirst, it's hard to recall.

The bus stop is a hundred yards from the street corner. A little crescent of shops sits back from the road, a green-grocer, a newsagent and a baker. In front of them, in the shade of a shallow arcade, stand a couple of buckets with flame dahlias, browning at the edges.

Patsy scans the first floor windows from the opposite side of the road. It is, she thinks, the flat above the greengrocer. The metal window frames there are freshly painted, exuberantly so, with the paint edging on to the glass. One window – the living room? – is open an inch or two, resting on its catch. She can't see, though; it's too bright in the sun, too dark inside. Her eyes travel along to the adjacent panel of bobbled glass where a bottle is visible. Dettol. Bathroom.

So which is the entrance? Between the baker and the greengrocer, she can make out a pair of numbers on a pale painted door. Inside something waits that he can never allow himself to be late for, yet it all looks so dismal. She has to adjust what she knows to what she sees, like easing her dress over her hips, wriggling to make it lie flat.

In the baker's window, she catches sight of the reflection of the most beautiful woman he has ever seen, standing squinting across the road; the bows on her shoes point inwards. The hair he has praised for its chic and volume and cut appears bleached to white in the sunlight. She is stranded there, not wanting to retreat, not able to go forward. There is only one person who can rescue her – the man who enthuses over her "sex appeal", who marvels at her body, who praises her sense of humour and warmth and who has suddenly withdrawn all his enthusiasm – and she would die rather than have him see her there.

And in an hour the children must be collected from school. And that is what she must do. That is what she will do.

The trick with the tree trunks is to keep them cool. Otherwise, warns Patsy, as she manoeuvres the plates from the middle shelf of the fridge, they'll go all floppy. The girls watch suspiciously as she lowers their miniature gardens on to the kitchen table. Sally's is not much more than a pile of daisy heads beside a sward of moss, but it has panache. Lucy has snipped, sieved and combed a tiny vegetable plot, the earth studded with carrot tops fashioned from spring onion stalks. Cocktail stick bean poles support tendrils of convulvulus. The Plasticene tree bears cotoneaster leaves and opalescent red berries which may well be poisonous. An accompanying handwritten note warns of the possibility. It will all add to the excitement of the competition. Won't it? says Patsy.

On the village green the fête is barely alive. The stalls are set out in a horseshoe. Single pastel figures drift from table to table, checking labels on jars and lining up counters on weathered games whose rules only a handful of the village residents understand.

They deliver the little gardens to the tent. The apple tree keels in the stale breath beneath the canvas. Noxious fruits drop on to the soil. Blinking outside in the light, the children look around, eager for events to overtake them. Lucy would like to look at the ponies for the pony rides, but not actually ride one. Sally might, though. Jimmy reckons the coconut shy will be easy-peasy.

Out of the heat haze figures have solidified into queues and knots curling from the stalls and tables. Beneath the farmyard noises of the band tuning up comes a sound altogether more persistent and disconcerting. It yodels and growls, drawls and croons.

It is all shook up, and then again, within an instant, yours for one night. It resonates with a muffled intensity.

"What's that?" squints Lucy, looking up at Patsy.

"I have *no* idea," responds her mother, squeezing her daughter's hand, trying to ward off any apprehension, "doesn't it sound funny? Shall we go and have a look?"

"It's a man in a box – how stupid, a man in a box!" Jimmy hits his forehead with the heel of his hand at the inanity of adults. "I don't believe it's . . . a man in a box."

"But what's he doing?"

"Well, he's singing. In a way. Let's go to see why he's in the box, shall we?" And they approach the Human Juke Box in his corrall. A slicked-down youth sits behind a table, taking the sixpences. Propped against the table leg a small blackboard bears half a dozen hit parade options and a couple of sentimentally Celtic standards. The juke box stands on drainpipe legs of grey flannel and his painted cardboard sides heave with the effort. As he shifts weight on pointed boots, the mellow voice lures and promises and teases, pouring out of the wonky grille.

Patsy is enfolded by it. As the children edge around the enclosure to discern the precise structure of the box and the singer's method of entry, she stands fired by the song's close-range power. A flush creeps from her collarbones, fingers of red beneath the silky poppies on her dress. Her body makes tiny forays into the air between her and the voice. Right now, she could love this man.

In fact, she does already. Less than a week ago, she disappeared entirely into his embrace: his body in hers, but not his, and not hers, blended beyond identity, beyond responsibility. For a few lost minutes. She could surrender for good, right now, if the song would only go on. This is what she was born for. This is where she gets to be herself.

Then in the closing bars a hiccup reveals a lack of breathing control. The singer clears his throat and inclines forward in an attempt at a bow, making the painted rainbow on his headdress bob towards the grass. Robust chatter springs up about the next choice. Does he know "Blue Velvet"? Just the numbers on the board, madam. Shame, I love that one – are you sure, dear? He's sure, and the voice, although young, is gruff and glib. Does she want to be taken home again, Kathleen? Well . . . A husband persuades her, the sixpence spins into the plate and the Human Juke Box breathes in mightily, his boxed shoulders rising to the challenge.

Patsy turns away, annoyed at the turn in events. Sally and Lucy are watching the dog show contestants gather.

Jimmy is standing in the centre of the horseshoe, kicking at divots. From a table by the Scout hut comes a low industrial grinding sound. A battered silver metal drum has begun to rotate and two or three figures are bending over it, peering in. They raise their voices to debate the operation. What is that? asks Jimmy, the lucky dip? Together the girls swing their heads and stop mid-step.

"I think," begins Patsy, faltering as the realization hits her. "Oh, yes. I think that must be the candyfloss."

"Gosh," says Jimmy. "Will you be in charge of that? Really?"

"Well, I expect someone else will actually operate the machinery. But I'll probably hand it out. You know."

"I wish I could do it – the engine bit. I'd make it go really fast."

They wander over for a look. On the table beside the metal bowl are brown paper bags of sugar and piles of pale wooden sticks. Small bottles of red food colouring are mustered like chess pieces. The bowl is gurgling round to a halt; the legs of the collapsible table tremble in sympathy.

Mrs Hopkins. The red-faced men beam at her, the first volunteer on the afternoon's roster. Just working out how exactly, don't want to get that lovely dress dirty. All up and running in a minute. Just bear with us. And she does as one of them pours sugar into the dark maw and another arms himself with a wooden stick. The third flicks the switch at the base of the apparatus and it clears its throat aggressively, sending particles of sugar spinning up in the air and into the eyes of the onlookers. They flinch and blink.

"Steady on," growls one. "Steady, the Buffs." No, no, they dispute the operational order. Rotate first and then pour – or perhaps simultaneously. And the colour – no point in candyfloss unless it's pink, eh? Frowning with intent, they lock into dialogue over the number of drops. The carmine falls from the bottle between them, creeping across the crystals. The bloodied mass churns into action and flings itself against the wall of death. Concerned, they watch its progress. It fails to transubstantiate. The smell of burning toffee is acrid.

"Let's clear that up, shall we?" smiles Patsy, threateningly. Oh yes, yes, best to do that, they concede, backing off. She picks out the hot twisted sugar mass in a tea towel and lays it discreetly by the empty boxes behind the table. She takes another cloth and wipes residue from the inside of the drum.

"Now," the children exchange glances and group themselves around one end of the table. Patsy pushes a strand of hair out of her eyes. "Turn on first, I think," she eyes the men, smiles brightly at their entreaties to be careful and flicks the switch. The machine gyrates with the uneven grace of a Hula-Hoop. Its gargling roar settles into a rhythm. With one hand, Patsy tips sugar in a fine stream into the centre of the rotating bowl. For nearly a minute, nothing happens. Eyebrows are raised in expectation (and judgement) and then Jimmy begins to shout.

"Look," he yells, making everyone jump, "look, there's something." They all peer further over the edge, except the little girls who squirm with frustration, held back by a cautious adult. The shadows cast by the circle of heads make it difficult to see. "I'm sorry," declares Patsy, "but there's really only room for one person to be in charge here and, since it seems to be me, I wonder if you would all stand back, please." They do.

There is nothing to see, or rather she finds she can see nothing at the bottom of the bowl, where once she saw dull silver. A fuzziness has softened the dents and scratches on the metal. Patsy picks up a stick and dips it tentatively into the spinning void. She yanks it back up, like a novice angler, and there on the tip of the wood is a fine net of creamy gold, a glistening mesh of spun sugar.

A triumphant exhalation runs around the group, but Patsy has plunged again into the whirling caramelized air. She stirs the wand around, rolling it between her fingers as she does, avoiding the sides of the cauldron, and weaves from the warmth and the sweetness and the speed a skein fat enough to wrap around the stick. When she feels it start to topple over, heavy with its puffy burden, she straightens her back and pulls the stick clear. Brandishing the staff aloft, she gives one final twist to secure the loose lock of candyfloss that hangs down like part of a barmaid's beehive towards the end of the evening.

"Oh, well done," they applaud, "splendid."

"Splendidly pale, though," says Patsy. "Can I trust one of you gentlemen to colour the sugar for me? I'm sure you can," she adds, with a mischievous touch.

The queue forms quickly. Patsy masters the technique

of wrapping a sheaf of candyfloss high and wide. Tiny pink fibres fly from the drum and adhere to her arms, curling as they cool around the fine golden hairs. Within minutes she notes the first trace on her fringe. Fathers of the children's friends fancy their skill with the drum, but all fail in a crackle of splintering sticks and congealed toffee. Patsy adopts a brisk tone with them. They settle for watching her. One, a dark man whom she has spotted in a two-tone Hillman, notes the candy fuzz on her skin, like a halo he says, and offers to remove it. He'll even pay full price. There is porky, abashed laughter. "I think we'll stick with the conventional method," she retorts. "For now."

Halfway down the queue, the cottage loaf that is Fred Rookin appears. He watches her performance appreciatively. Emboldened by the crowd and the attention she beams at him. "Mr Rookin," she calls, "Mr Rookin, do you think this will be a useful skill to have in the United States? Do you think there'll be much call for it?"

"They will find you, Mrs Hopkins, entirely accomplished, I have no doubt. I am full of admiration." Rookin is frowning slightly and she is struck suddenly by the truth of his tone, in the midst of the noise and the stickiness.

"Oh nonsense." She gives a little laugh. "Just getting on with it." She is embarrassed at his obvious kindness. The assembled admirers are waiting for her comment. After all she has hauled him up before them all for some kind of sport. She's that kind of girl, evidently.

Rookin is contemplating his brown slip-on shoes; the sun throws shadows into his pitted skin.

"Oh, you'll be away from us soon. Leaving us all behind. We'll watch your meteoric rise."

Patsy takes a sudden breath. She puts a hand on the spinning rim of the candyfloss machine to steady it. The metal is hot, but the pain is welcome because it gives purpose to the hot tears surging against her lower lids.

"I must say, Mrs Hopkins," adds Rookin, confidentially, deferentially even, "how very gratifying – and reassuring – it is to see you looking so much yourself once more." She acknowledges this confidence with a nod, bending down to scoop air and sugar. "I was a little worried for a while. We all were." And he smiles briefly and then turns his attention, with a distinct brightening, towards the airy confection that is whirling itself up for him.

I hate farewells. I never manage them. Sometimes I just leave and then I telephone afterwards, which is hardly the honourable route. For me the process of leave-taking is too obvious a reminder. For all we know, we may never meet again. And not only do I not say goodbye until the very last minute, when I do I know I am sometimes brusque, although I cry also.

There were tears certainly, on my part at least, when Patricia left with the children. Who knew how big they would be when they returned, how different? Poor Lucy was very distraught and apprehensive, but little Sally, of course, was cheerful. And obstinate, no need to worry about her. And James, very grown up. The man of the house. You know.

Patricia was not her usual self those last few days. Very subdued, lethargic almost. It was as if she had fought the difficulties of the move, of the separation from Alan, and then, at the very end of it all, she was exhausted. Almost resigned, although I'm not sure what about, because this move – she'd said it so many times – was such an opportunity for them.

And all that toing and froing from the house had finally come to an end. No more trucks manoeuvring around that tight corner in the Close; no more visits from the man from Alan's company, whose name I forget, or from his chauffeur, his assistant, the beautiful boy, always there with some piece of paper for Patsy to sign. No more builders, those builders who'd made such a mess of that fireplace. Extraordinary. I would have been so angry, I was so angry when I saw it, but she just shrugged and changed the subject. She must have been relieved when they all left her to tidy up her life on her own.

I did think that, before she left, she was really looking forward to seeing her husband again. I seem to remember a conversation when she talked about him, for the first time that I can recall, without embarrassment. Maybe she even said the word love. People did, you know, even then. For some reason – and who knows what goes on between husbands and wives? – she no longer appeared angry with him.

And I have a very vivid image of her, just before they left, at one of those funny summer occasions, a fête worse than death, as Donald always said, without fail. And always without fail it made me laugh. She was very tired, Patricia, but someone had persuaded her to help with a stall, selling something, sweets of some kind. She was handing them out, I think, and there was a queue. It was an attraction in itself – maybe some kind of game. And all the men, well, they lined up for some of her special attention, a sprinkling of gold dust. Donald, of course, he was an easy target. He was so devoted to her; he would put on his best linen jacket, so distinguished, when he knew he would see her. So, he joined this queue, all expectant, and there were already many there and she was pale but smiling at everyone – and at no one in particular.

I watched her – after all, everyone else was doing that, including my husband – and after a few minutes she seemed to get stronger, a little less fragile. It was almost as though her admirers expected her to dazzle, and she was glad of the challenge, grateful for it. For a moment, it was a kind of balance. Patricia had hit her stride again, I think that's what they say about horses, isn't it? That man from the Company, the big one, middle-aged, he said something about her being a pioneer, showing us all the way. I don't know about that. Maybe, you know, she was just happy that she was going to see her man again. I would have been. He was a good man, Alan. I think. I suppose.

I sat at one of the little tables where they served tea – always that English tea, lukewarm with heavy cake, which

I never touched – and I watched. The sun was dropping a little, but the air was heating up, the way it does in August. The red flowers on Patsy's dress stood out, the dress itself had a sheen. So clever, I remember thinking, the way those new fabrics could lock in colour and lustre; they could stretch and ruffle and then cling. Anything you wanted and then, in a trice, new every day. And now look at them, not pretending to be silk or wool or cotton anymore, just proud to be some highly technical formula or like skin – out on a spaceship or back in the cave. One or the other.

Everyone was doing what they should; the sun was shining; the little band played; somebody pinned a ribbon on to the dog most like its owner; little Lucy won a sewing set for her garden on a plate – very neat, very pretty. And Patricia was everyone's dream – even her own.

Or maybe I remember it like this, because it's a time that's burnished, you know, I've looked after it in my memory. We wouldn't go to many more of these occasions, and none I think as special as this one. In a few years, four maybe five, it would be Donald's last August out and about, and, in a sense, mine too. One of the last summers when he . . . well, you know, I don't really want to dwell on all that. It's funny to think that we were married for less time than Patricia and Alan. My marriage ended before theirs did, I suppose, technically. But we know that's a nonsense, don't we? After all I'm really still married, after all these years.

15

SOMETIME AT the end of the century, when he's Lavenirre Professor (emeritus) at a prestigious and airy textile college in the Bible-belt South, Alan will have cause to consider scar tissue. From his comfortable position (a handful of lectures a year, no need even to keep a house down there and as much consultancy as he can schedule into his cross-talking electronic diaries) he'll have the leisure at last to ponder some of the notions that have so amused his colleagues over the years. The Golden Age of synthetic fibres will be well over, exhausted in the mid-eighties by a combination of competition from emerging economies and a certain decadence in home-grown research. No doubt about it, the early sixties were just the best time. Exciting? Gosh, yes. Alan will never lose that "gosh", just as he'll never renounce his British passport; for later generations of students, weaned on Turner Classic Movies, this will endow him with a certain

Jimmy Stewart period appeal. They'll even suspect that, like Jimmy, Alan's niceness is a veneer for steel or possibly something nastier. Gosh, yes.

The trouble is, Alan will tell them, the incentive to innovate drops away. Sharply. For a while, decades even, competitors strive to invent. The prizes are so great, it's worth the effort. After a while though, you find a product that's pretty good, does much of what everyone wants; the race then is to produce it in bulk, at the lowest unit cost. We're talking polyester here, he adds for the ones at the back, or down front, with the shiny padded jackets and the blank faces. Not so much incentive to find something new, because if you do, it's purely for a niche market. High cost to develop, got to be a high return. It's like cars. If I can invent an overcoat that breathes sweat out and kills odour (he'll smile when they write this down, or fiddle with the volume on their hand-held recorders; he will have repeated it so many times over the years that its painful connotations have faded) but won't let rain in, then I can sell that at over a thousand dollars to those types picking over Machu Picchu in July.

Alan will be executing an arduous tour of duty on the tourist trail himself. He'll owe it to his second wife; she will insist on their discovering places to discover together, on new sets of memories. His most rewarding hours, however, will be spent in his study with the spectacular desert view, thinking the unthinkable, as he'll call it.

So one afternoon he'll pick abstractedly over a wide wooden dish of shells and other beach detritus thoughtfully placed by his wife at the side of his single-slice white oak writing table. Bring back that heaven in the Turks and Caicos, sweetheart, she will have said, still not realizing that bliss for him remains a blank piece of paper plus time. That afternoon, he'll rub a tiny blueish crab claw between his right thumb and forefinger for minutes while he makes notes with the left hand. Eventually, pausing on the headland of some premise, he'll look down at the pincer and the chalky break in the shell where it parts company with the body. He'll sniff at it, to summon up the ocean, but even as he does, he'll consider its solidity and durability, but also its flexibility, its permeability and lack of toxicity. If you could only . . . he'll wonder, for his thoughts inevitably will be woven through with the medical morality tales of his contemporaries, if you could only simulate this in spare part surgery. Or if not simulate, maybe synthesize . . .?

The old excitement will spark, the phone ring, the fax wheeze and the e-mails slide into view with a bullish fanfare. He won't carry out the research himself, of course, but he'll consult and confer and generally take a paternal interest. He'll inform himself about physiology; the process of healing, for example, how you graft a synthetic organ or vein on to the framework that once supported the diseased one without accumulating layers of obstructive tissue. He'll become familiar with the Young Turks of immunology: he'll ponder the body's response to certain irritants. One evening, as they'll sit on the deck, looking beyond the adobe changing suite by the pool to the purple shadows stretching across the rocky volcanic plugs, his second wife will remark with her laborious humour on the emotional resonance of his work. Scar tissue, she'll say, that's what I deal in too.

And he won't think of her status as supervisor to a web of specialist counsellors in workplace-induced marital stress from Boston to Washington. He'll think of Patsy.

There are moments, he'll consider, staring at the weave of his linen trousers through the almond pallor of a glass of Pinot Grigio, when it could all have gone the other way. They started out so well in America. He'll remember. He'll recall. He'll summon up phrases and images, entire conversations which will remain as clear as yesterday to him, he who can never remember his daughters' birthdays. But they want to forget them too, these days, he'll proffer in defence. As if he'd ever remembered. It will be true that his memories will be somewhat distorted by the exhaustive rehearsal that his second wife will have demanded. She will be so anxious not to repeat any futile pattern; they must continue to progress, to grow together. She will need to identify where exactly his marriage to Patsy failed.

Looking into the deep sky above him, he'll think of all those digital conversations, the cellular phone exchanges and broadcasts, that linger out there. All that talk and no context. How would it be to hear those conversations again? Even the early analogue ones; especially those. Maybe you could trace a trajectory.

Occasionally, on the maid's night off, when he's alone

in the house, when his second wife is away supervising her pyramid of counsellors, or pushing back her auburn mane to dedicate copies of that singularly successful book of hers to anxious women in Barnes & Noble with stressed, flat hair, then he pours a proscribed scotch (all spirits are forbidden by Shulamith on his new regime) and turns up the sound system so loud that the water trembles on the surface of the Japanese garden. Then he puts away his wife's Diana Krall and selects only the old stuff. Not all of it has been digitally remastered and, although he's something of a purist in sound these days, there's a thrill from hearing the hiss and crackle of an original Capitol recording. (He has recalled some conversation, way back, in Ray Daniels' house, about the idea of digital recording. Old Ray called that one wrong, didn't he? Poor old Ray.) Each time he plays it, he hears something new, a key change in a ballad or a catch in the singer's voice during one of her oh-so-formal introductions. He has wondered occasionally if, in fact, this particular recording is actually a compilation of several live appearances; the applause hiccups occasionally, evidence of sound edits; the whole performance is not exactly as he remembers it.

There was an expression popular in business circles in the eighties. Briefing himself before a trip to a foreign sub-sidiary or partner, he'd stress to the research boys the importance of "hitting the ground running". Vietnam in origin, he supposed, or Korea more likely.

When she reached the States, Patsy was already at full sprint. The house, naturally, was licked into shape in no time, but her customary enthusiasm for interiors seemed to have faded. She was limited, perhaps, by it being rented accommodation.

What Patsy did was join. She encouraged Alan to take up the company introduction to the country club, she volunteered for swim patrol, she learnt golf with a group of young mothers all permitted under special licence to use the clubhouse on Tuesday afternoons. He doesn't remember quite when, but she acquired a new tone of voice to return the greetings of her new acquaintances. He could never have said Patsy was hearty, but she became somehow more "outdoors". The children, Jimmy in particular, were delighted.

Patsy taught herself to swim like an American, with bold overarm strokes. She'd practise in the mornings, after seeing the children on to the school bus. Before then, she'd hardly swum at all, wading gingerly into the shallows on family holidays and barely getting the skirt of her costume wet. On the rare occasions he was home in Bettesville in the morning, he remembered the rhythmic slap of her hand hitting the end of the pool and the rush of water as she set off again for another length. Locked behind her white goggles and flowered hat, she didn't invite interruption. At weekends she'd challenge Jimmy to race her, until she could match him over five lengths. Then she seemed to relax and let Jimmy overtake her. Sally was fearless in the water, jumping "atom bombs" into the deep end, but Lucy stayed with her head firmly above water, clinging to the old duck rubber ring they'd brought from England, searching with one foot for the sloping floor.

One evening he came home and found Patsy squatting beside the water, with a tearful Lucy holding on to the side. Why, he heard her say, why can't you do it? I did it. Just get on with it, Lucy. Please. It's not difficult. Just do it.

Perhaps he should have said something, but he wasn't sure he should intervene right then. After all, he didn't really know what was going on.

There were photographs somewhere – who knows which member of the family has them now? – which show Patsy as he remembers her from that time. Bobbed hair, a white head band, a distinct glow on the tanned cheekbones, her eyes hidden away in a wide, wide smile. And always a nifty golfing skirt, or Bermuda shorts for the trampolining sessions that were the current craze. Were they really? One night as she climbed into bed he saw the gentle definition of calf muscles, the first time he'd seen anything so blatant on her trim form.

A couple of years into their time there together, she grew her hair longer. He liked it that way best of all. Men always do, he supposes. She'd rather given up on the tennis and the golf, or at least on the people who went with it. A few of the brighter ones were still guests at the parties they held, regularly, at the house. When he became a vice-president, and director of Innovative

Research (as if there *were* another kind), they moved up to the Hill, neo-colonial, with a bigger pool. Patsy preferred the architecture, she said, reminded her more of Europe. OK, she'd admitted to him one night, maybe not a Europe we know particularly, but culturally it just feels right.

Locally, Patsy had become the expert on Europe. For many people, she was it, one and the same, Britannia and Marianne and Brunnhilde and Tosca all in one. No one ever listened to Alan's protests that she was so English. She held a local monopoly on chic. They did entertain "in the European style", it was true. French provincial became her forte. And the fringe and the piled-up hair gave her a passing resemblance to a more mature Bardot. She pioneered those checked bikinis in Delaware. We feel, their guests sometimes remarked, as though we've just taken a European vacation.

He glimpsed her once, barefoot and wearing only that gingham bikini, carrying a tray of food from the kitchen into the sun lounge for the chattering crowd of colleagues and neighbours. By that time her hair was a kind of stripey blonde, he supposes, and her eyelashes long and dark. He remembers the line of her cheekbones and seeing, as one might spot a chromatic pattern, that curve repeated in her lowest ribs and in the long muscles of her thighs. She was smiling out at their guests and then her eyeline flickered sideways down the corridor in his direction and the smile lost its force. He saw her eyes getting older, accentuated by the false eyelashes. For a moment, he wished he could dismiss all these outsiders and take her into some inner part of the house and tell her how very beautiful she was. But the house didn't have any such sanctuary.

She worried, he sometimes thought, all the more when fêted for success. Her anxiety would find another channel. Jimmy always did well at school; he's always had a positive enquiring outlook, but Lucy had problems from the start. In fact, it was Patsy's determination to help her, to chivvy her along (he stops short of the term "bully" because he means it only in the most benign sense) that led to Patsy enrolling in classes herself. One spring, he recalls with a smile, she "bagged" the Major Composers in the Liberal Arts (Music) morning courses at the state university. Next semester it was Art History. The dining room table was covered in heavy books on Veronese and Andrea del Sarto. It will help Lucy with her Western Civilization classes, Patsy assured him. He's not sure how much of it actually helped Lucy at the time, although, now he thinks about it, Lucy did eventually make her career in furniture restoration. So some of that aesthetic stuff must have rubbed off.

Patsy found a new group of friends, older women mostly, earnest widows and retired career girls. Not so much fun, he observed at the time. Fun? She wasn't impressed by that; she was fired with the importance of education. We owe it to the children, she said, it's their heritage. They deserve an English education. He remembers arguing with her that there seemed little point:

their future was obviously here and if not in Delaware then elsewhere in America. Jimmy adored the American life; by the age of fourteen or fifteen he'd set his heart on science and MIT in particular. The girls had made friends, they'd do fine.

It was a shock when she continued to disagree. No, he has to concede, and it isn't easy, it was painful. He wasn't brought up to do this kind of thing, but his second wife has taught him over the years. Very painful to discover that, for the first time in their married life, Patsy and he didn't share a view of the road ahead. America had become his life. Well, look at him – where else could have given him all this? But she wanted to go home.

So much of their married life from then on was conducted on the phone, it seems to him now. Maybe it started even earlier. From the first conversations, Delaware to Springfield Drive, metered for length, he felt the frustration of it. It was like a race, the first few exchanges and then they'd be off.

Going right back to the beginning, he was sorry he hadn't been the one to tell her about the move to America in the first place. Or even earlier, that he hadn't explained what his first trip might mean, properly. That old fool Rookin had got in first, delighted with the importance of the task. He'd told the children too, which was less than perfect. From the outset, in those phone conversations, always with that bloody delay, Patsy had put up every objection she could. She seemed obsessed with the practicalities – schooling, making new friends, packing up for the move. She threw up objections, she worried about decisions they might never have to make. He has the impression of sitting in a bright office in the early afternoon nearly forty years ago, with one eye on the clock, conscious that his three-minute units are running out fast. The line was noisy, which seemed to alarm her, there was a delay and he was trying to jolly her along. Using blunt shears to cut canvas.

The irony was, when the time came, she was the one who really seemed to throw herself into the new life. As he knew she would. He keeps coming back to this. Their plans had always worked out; it just took a little time because they wanted to do things better than most people. He thought she understood this. He thought she understood that everything he was doing, all those years for the Company, were for her and the children.

Look, he said at the end of one of those early transatlantic conversations, exasperated, don't you miss me at all? He doesn't quite remember what she said. Of course. Don't be silly. I'll give the children hugs for you.

Something like that.

The nature of memory has begun to interest Alan. He has very few photographs of that period before they moved to America. Patsy probably has what still exists of those early days, but she's the last to keep anything on display; he is sometimes shocked by how unsentimental she appears. Lucy tells him in her usual wry manner that it's because she's such a romantic, such an idealist, that she can't bear the inadequacies of photography and, anyway, her mother is horrified that in one of those early snaps she looks a little like Myra Hindley. Alan finds this apparent vanity – or delicacy – endearing. When you consider what a formidable matriarch she has become.

He has tried to get together with Patsy: he would like, with an urgency he can't altogether rationalize, to reconstruct a common version of their marriage and its decline. But she's having none of it. Her version was laid down in the 1970s, when she grew that leonine hair. (It was the fashion, like feminism. He can't help it, but he still prefers the Bardot look.) In this common version (he believes, for he's relying only on what his son and daughters tell him, and they in turn make of their accounts anecdotes, embroidering and shaping for entertainment, taste and decency), there was a period of enlightenment when she shook off the chains of domesticity and was enfranchized by education. Oh, come on, Alan chuckles, and the children smirk too. She doesn't really believe she was enslaved, with all the gadgets and advantages of life in America, does she? She could always do whatever she wanted.

Once, recently, he visited Lucy at her home in England, near Worcester. All the way along the M5, as the driver took instructions from the terse female voice on his route planner screen, Alan stored up the questions he wanted to ask Lucy about her mother. Lucy is the only child who'll talk about her, really.

When he got to the cottage (he supposes it's a cottage, pretty small in his judgement) he was overwhelmed by the damp warmth of the kitchen and the small children with red cheeks from the cold and runny noses. He reckons they're not that well off, but Lucy laughed at his suggestion of a cash injection. Dad, we're fine.

At dinner, he was too busy reacting to all the news about Toby's nursery class or Yseult's (Izzy, of course) ballet lessons. Wonderful, how they manage all that out here, he thought, looking at the skeleton trees through the uncurtained window. I will get round to it; I've bought the material, Lucy sighs. One day.

Later, Mark left for his stint at the Samaritans. We can tell you, said Lucy, but we have to keep quiet to everyone else. In a rural area, with a relatively small population, there's a fair chance you'll know the person on the other end of the line or at least their family. Wonderful service, says Alan, with genuine admiration, not able to keep his eyes off the old rug tacked across the window.

With the children asleep, he and Lucy sat by the wood–burner in the little front room for an hour or so until his driver came to take him to the hotel. At last, he could ask about Patsy. She smiled conspiratorially. He knows she sees her regularly, the only one of the children who does, the only one in the same country.

And is she happy? He knew the question was heavy handed. Lucy looked at him sympathetically. Then she

said the strangest thing, as she opened the door of the
wood stove and shoved another log in. It was almost
aggressive. She said Patsy once told her that he couldn't
love her the way she wanted to be loved, in her soul.
Nonsense, he spluttered. I adored her: she just didn't give
me the chance. God knows, I put up with enough, I could
tell you. She got to be quite out of hand, your mother.
Oh, don't, Daddy, said Lucy. Spare me the thought of
Mummy at full tilt.

There *are* some photographs. He thinks Lucy must have
them somewhere, although he's not sure where you'd
find them under the old newspapers and children's toys
and tools from Lucy's work area. These would be photos
of the family in America during the time when Patsy and
Alan became Al and Pat, host and hostess. In the European
style. Her hair was long then, and straight. She *was*
beautiful, he told Lucy that same evening, all that hair
worn loose and her skin tanned from those afternoons by
the pool. Great figure for a mother of three, but then she
never stopped, barely sat down.

Often taken for your sister, remember Luce? Some of
those young boys who came to the house in England later
when you were a teenager, well they hardly knew which
one to ogle, eh?

Thanks Dad, says Lucy, glumly. Sorry my love, he says.
I wonder what they'd think of her now, all those
computer consultants or whatever they became.

The ones who'd joined film club, they'd think she'd turned into Jeanne Moreau. Later Jeanne Moreau, that is, ventures Lucy, smiling a little now.

In the end, you know, he told her, the decision to return the family to Britain was one we both made. Oh, right, she says. I'll bet.

Well, we reached some kind of agreement, he concedes. We were getting to that crossroads in Jimmy's education. Your Mum felt that sixth form and first degree courses were superior in Britain. She was probably right, anyway. And we still owned that house in Springfield Drive, although obviously we needed something bigger by then. And I've never understood why exactly she wanted to go back to a provincial town with a godawful climate. Nice enough place, though.

Of course, to be hard-headed about it, Alan has to admit he was away so much himself at the time that he was only in Delaware a week or so a month. That was the way business was going, alliances and partnerships with manufacturers in the East. You had to keep your eye firmly on the opposition. He'd started to live in planes, and cartoon vapour trails spelled London as easily as New York, Chicago or Tokyo. It was the Jet Age. *Boeing Boeing*. No great problem then, if he had to divide his time. Not an equal division, admittedly, so when he did eventually catch up with the family either in person, or more frequently on the phone, he *was* always catching up. Time delay.

Maybe that was why, whenever he made a topical joke

(finding oil off Great Yarmouth, if that really happened, the World Cup getting stolen, that sort of thing), they seemed slow to catch on. Oh Dad, your jokes – you were never one of life's natural comedians, Lucy said. We didn't have the faintest idea what you were going on about.

When I got to speak to you at all, he said. Television began to suck you all in more – and in the new, bigger house there was more space to be sucked into. Don't interrupt *Thunderbirds*, or *Top of the Pops* or *Get Smart*. I'll get them to call you later, she'd say. And sometimes you did. When he thinks back, Patsy wasn't so easy to track down herself, not once she was away at the evening classes, and then the part-time university course, after Jimmy had left for Leeds. Didn't she start with some kind of Civic Studies, before the Law? He remembers her making a remark about acclimatizing again when he wondered what she wanted to do Civic Studies for.

Acclimatizing, he said, shifting the old armchair a little closer to the stove. Patsy never wanted to acclimatize. She couldn't help it: she had to stand out.

Those years fold back on themselves; he has a little trouble with the chronology, but he can pin it to the big events – patents, mergers, acquisitions. The girls filled him in when he called about their schoolwork or Mum's exams. Did they feel neglected? He hopes not. They were proud of her, too. It was the early seventies. They were all reading the key feminist texts. Is it right that Sally claims that when she was thirteen she used to sneak into the school library at break times to read Germaine Greer, who was otherwise restricted to sixth formers?

She can't possibly have understood it, said Lucy, with a little of the old disapproval. His second wife was reading it at the same time, too, Alan said, part of her course work at Berkeley. And naturally even he's read it, now.

The house changed fast after Jimmy left for university, doesn't she think? In the end he had no alternative but to spend just a few days a month there. It was easier to work out of the serviced apartment in Bettesville, just two minutes from Head Office.

In any case, he said, trying hard not to let any grievance show, he always felt accommodated in that new house, rather than welcomed. He usually brought presents; his secretary had kids around the same age, so she'd put together a collection. I'm ashamed to say it, but what did I know then? You loved the music, even if you were a bit dismissive of the rest. Thanks, Dad, you and Sally would say, but I'm not really into all this commercial stuff. Commercial was the insult then.

Alan stopped himself from adding how ludicrous it seemed to him at the time; it's a little sad now, as though they never realized what he went through to school and feed and house them. But he'll have to live with it; he supposes they understand these days how the world works.

And Patsy became Patricia around then. She thought it was demeaning somehow, a diminutive. I'm not a girl any more, she told him. I'm not just Mummy's daughter. I prefer Patricia anyway. Is it a problem? No, not a problem, obviously it wasn't a problem. It just seemed ridiculous and frankly, as far as he was concerned, impossible. He was never going to remember.

He didn't get much opportunity, in any case.

And Lucy, he asks her, remembering the time, you are enjoying this furniture restoration, aren't you, sweetheart? I mean it's not too much for you, working like this at home with the children and stuff still to do on the house? And with so little help? You're OK living like this?

Suddenly he finds his eyes brimming with tenderness.

In the car driving away down the unmade track, he reflects on Lucy's kind of busyness. He and Patsy had a different way. In those telephone calls, he always made light of his schedule (perhaps too light) while she laboured hers. Once, she joked, he wouldn't last five minutes at her pace. The joke was followed by a sharp uppercut. I don't see why you bother to fly six thousand miles for a couple of days. Your life is over there or somewhere: mine's here. She sounded defiant, almost as if she wanted him to contradict her, but she was right. You could be here, he'd protested. Well, you wouldn't be there either, she said, like a small child. Is this what you want? he asked. Well, *this* isn't what I want, she said.

Sally was the only one left at home when the divorce came through. It's all right, Dad, she'd said, it was only a matter of time, wasn't it? He was horrified. Is his version of reality entirely untrustworthy?

There's a version he could construct in which he and Patsy meet, fall in love, fight, fall out of love and then part. That has the merit of logic. It's easier all round on all the protagonists. Alan's problem is that his version doesn't go like that. There is no moment he can point to where the edifice began to crumble. He's used the term "grown apart" for the twenty or so years since the divorce. Until he met Shulamith, who withheld her approval until he could bring her some offering of past pain. Grew apart in what sense, Alan? If our relationship is to have a chance, Alan, I need to know what went wrong. So he constructed a second version for her in which he is the unconscious villain, the absent spouse whose emotional niggardliness starved the relationship of its force. Alan, said Shulamith, you have to learn to forgive yourself for this. Let me help you.

And he would forgive himself, but it's hard when you can only find minor transgressions to absolve. Anyway, the important thing is to allow Shulamith to help him. He's glad that his second wife finds satisfaction in this version of his marriage to Patsy, but he is increasingly at sea. It was no worse, surely, than other people's marriages? Who knows, least of all the principals?

Just recently, he was in one of the local malls, searching for a small gift to add to the Seychelles trip he's giving Shulamith for her birthday. In between Banana Republic and Victoria's Secret, there's a small gallery which offers wooden bowls and painted glass, silverware and eccentric ceramics. Fourth-rate art, lurid daubs of Florida and Arizona, loiter on the walls. He wandered among the miniature models of old technology. A little typewriter in sterling silver? Fibre optics prostituted to table lamps? He found himself considering a genuine Navajo-design mouse-rug. Among the carousels of cards he saw one with two silhouettes, a photograph of a couple standing on a rocky promontory gazing down on a river that wound through a scrubby valley. An italicized aphorism beneath spelt out a message: love is not so much about gazing at one another as gazing together at the road ahead.

Alan stares at the card, frowning.

As he leaves the shop for the echoing walkways of the mall, his pocket is weighted with his eventual choice, a small medallion of an angel wrapped in Celtic scroll. A guardian for my travels, Shulamith will exclaim, suddenly sentimental. On his way out, Alan skirts the litter-strewn tables of young people downing greenapple Slush Puppies and eating felafel wraps, killing time.

One thing he remembers, like a perfect miniature, is the couple who lived across the close from them in the Springfield Drive house, Donald and Evie. Delightful people, although he always felt awkward around Donald. The poor chap had clearly messed up somewhere with his business, lost most of what he'd built up. Alan continues to find ineptitude a little unsettling; he has had so little experience of it in his professional life, or at least tolerated so little. It's different now with students – the great failing of democratic education, the lowest common denominator, just don't get him started. Donald and Evie, well, they were making the best of it, downscaling before their time. He did never quite understand, though, why Patsy held them in such affection. No, it wasn't just affection as such; it was as if she were in thrall to them a little, although there was no earthly reason why she should be. Quite the reverse. He found them, with their pristine doll's house and their billing and cooing, faintly ludicrous. He remembers it as embarrassing, all that teenage love-struck stuff at their age; they sometimes seemed to forget themselves. Strangely, that was when Patsy was at her most fascinated, as if she admired this self-forgetfulness. And now, here's the irony, he doesn't want her to forget anything, not herself and especially not the past. He wants her just the way she was.

But that's mad of course. He slings a cashmere sweater over his pure cotton shirt, presents both from his second wife, who sources only organic materials from environmentally dutiful producers. This scar tissue thing: it stops him, even now, having those conversations he'd like to have with Patsy. Patricia. Back then, there must have been a time when their every observation and gesture wasn't overlaid with the patina of old quarrels, when it was possible to be spontaneous. In retrospect, he rather savours the later complexity; it does at least suggest common experience. You have to care to fight like that –

and she was always a formidable opponent. He didn't think that at the time of course; he escaped from it, whenever he could, back into the certainties of work.

Oh, well. If the children badger her enough, Patricia will talk about those days. But it's so long ago. Another person, you know, she says. I'd really rather not. She can't admit to them that by the time they returned to England, the very thing that once made her desolate, Alan's absence, had become a vacation of sorts. Nothing much to worry about then, except the children.

And she does talk to their father, occasionally. They have the grandchildren in common, of course. But his life, ludicrous, don't you think? All that stuff – that was in part their downfall, all the stuff. She reflects in her old cottage in the wild Somerset garden (find a seat if you can, darling, just plonk those books down on the floor and don't the foxgloves look *wonderful*, yes, just behind you, there) gently nudging them towards her academic achievements. It wasn't easy; she doesn't think they ever realize what a struggle it was, running the family and being a student – with only the occasional phone call from the lord and master. Who, frankly, didn't have a clue.

Well, maybe she does know that she is a little *difficult* about this. Maybe not entirely honest, but what's the point of dragging it all up again, now? What purpose would it serve? And they've both been happy, subsequently, whatever that means, not unhappy anyway.

She smiles through the dimpled glass at the latest man, retired teacher or doctor, DIY expert invariably, as he prunes the apple trees or mends the guttering. He might be returning from town, unloading plastic bags of provisions from the old Volvo. Practical men, they are, and quiet. She looks at whichever child it is – Lucy usually, but Jimmy sometimes, rarely Sally – as if to challenge them. Well?

(I don't know why she does that, Lucy tells Sally over the phone later. I find it touching, about the only thing about her I ever have found touching. This tenderness towards these chaps; it's almost as if she's discovered that love and pity can go together. That it might even be better that way.

Or perhaps they just don't answer back, says Sally.)

Soon their mother returns to the old tack. It's not so much of a short cut to say that Alan really wanted her to stay in the kitchen. Well, OK, it is an irony that he began to take so many holidays when he married again, and to a so-called professional woman. Although it's not what she'd call a profession. But it's typical of the kind of pasteurized, synthesized existence he's chosen. Stop exchanging glances, she tells them. At least I went out and did a job that contributed to intellectual life in some way. She waves behind her at the journals. Absolutely, they say, quite an achievement.

She's put on a bit of weight recently. Her hair is still thick and shiny, steely silver. Her wrists are weighed down with silver bangles.

And what can she tell them? Of the terrible silences in those phone conversations when she could have reached out, maybe, and made it better? That she dared herself to wait, because the silence was exquisite in its awfulness, and he might, *might* just do something that would sweep all the doubt away? That there was a time when all that seemed a bit of a game?

And the children notice, when they mention Alan's name, that her hand moves nervously to the back of her head, as if tidying the strands of some earlier, more formal style.

Patricia. The children have called her that for years; Lucy says her little girl Izzy, the first grandchild, does so too. So he's gradually learning. Patricia currently lives alone, he believes. She's had various romantic attachments over the years, most of them (so he's surmised) a little younger than her. None of them, he notes with a trace of satisfaction of which he is immediately ashamed, appeared to bring her any lasting happiness.

Ah well, Dad, that's because she has such deep expectations of romance, said Sally mischievously, when he managed to corral all three of the children for dinner for Jimmy's thirty-fifth. Does she? Does she? he'd flailed about. Oh shut up, Sal, she's the most unromantic romantic I've ever encountered, said Lucy. Anyway, maybe she likes her happiness in short doses. Though it does take a certain determination to be as hopeful as that, over and over again.

Sally had snorted. They were sitting out in southern California, looking down on the lights from some hilltop temple of cuisine. He'd paid for Lucy's ticket, but she was spending most of her time worrying about the children. Jimmy was looking prosperous and fit, but keeping a little aloof from the girls' bickering. He doesn't really have time for that kind of thing.

That night, Alan had looked at Sally and for the first time spotted the physical resemblance. Her hair was short, and reddish blonde. She was wearing a black suit, very neat and cool, Armani probably. She was a lawyer too, but real estate. Back in Colorado, there was a partner, a plump little woman who kept house and wrote unpublished poetry. They were all a little frightened of Sally.

All the same, Lucy said, then, surprising even herself, I do worry about Mum. The table fell silent. Each time he'd reined in his disapproval at reports of the energy and vigour some fresh liaison had sparked in Patricia. ("She looks amazing, Dad, about twenty years younger. Really. And she makes jokes. Not particularly funny ones, but she's trying.") Then, a year or two on, she'd swing away to be alone for a while, reinventing herself. She's always been good at that, consistent in it, you might say.

From perfect wife to bright socializer to worthy lawyer to grand old campaigner. Still rearranging the furniture.

In short, there had been – so far as he could make out – no relationship that had replaced theirs in magnitude. She was happy to have malleable chaps she could boss around until she bored of them. Whereas he . . . he had all this. Or perhaps that was simply his ego at work again. Anyway, it suited the children to see Patricia happy in her restless way. But could he trust their version of events? Could he trust hers? He can't trust his own.

In lectures he gives about the history of synthetic fibres in the post-war period, Alan often makes reference to the Harvesting Period. That's where we are now, he says, and he notices blinking and stirring at this point among the students as they sniff the home straight, it's the time when an industry takes what it can while it can, exploiting its arsenal of products before the Next Big Thing comes along. The bad news for you people, he adds, is that the best for synthetic textiles is probably behind us. Dinosaurs like me enjoyed all the action. They don't usually laugh much, his audience, but then it isn't a joke.

What am I harvesting now? Alan wonders, sitting at his pale oak desk, watching the points of solar-powered lamps in the darkened garden. Stories? Ideas? Things that made my heart beat faster?

Patricia knows exactly when she knew it must end. She has a fidelity to that moment, as she does to her first glimpse of Alan in the student hall more than forty years ago. Perhaps it's an arbitrary sort of fidelity. Even she would concede that the two moments in themselves did

not at the time seem particularly weighted with significance. In the second case she didn't act on the
revelation immediately, or indeed for several years. She
needs a structure to the narrative, though, and she chooses
to remember this particular conversation as pivotal.
Someone else, her former husband, for example, might
not have given it a second thought, but she remembers
this telephone call very clearly, almost word for word. She
remembers remembering it, anyway.

It may seem so clear because it was held in public – on
a public phone, in fact. The call box was wedged between
a red marble pillar and the kind of institutional painted
wall where you can smell the lead in the paint. Shiny but
scratched, a kind of custard-yellow that fought against the
red. For once, it wasn't a transatlantic call. Alan was only
ten miles away or so, at their home. If he'd ever lived
there, that is, then it might have been their home.

She was in the foyer of the County Hospital, somewhere between the coffee and tea machine and the little
cart offering faded orange and pink dahlias. The foyer
echoed with footsteps. Doors swung and banged on
squeaky hinges. Her hand holding the spare change was
pressed against her ear. She can remember the sweaty
metal smell of the coins. She would not, as it turned out,
need them all.

Maybe if he hadn't said that thing about Jimmy. He'd
just collected Jimmy from chess club, an arrangement that
required a detailed map and several phone calls. Jimmy's
school was a foreign country to Alan. He's really very

good, you know, and there's this big match on Saturday, said Alan. She knew that; she'd told him the night before. Alan wouldn't still be here on Saturday anyway. Of course, he'd said, crestfallen. Well then, he'd said, what else do I have to tell you?

He had suddenly sounded bewildered. Don't, she thought. Don't be lost, she wanted to scream. Help me. In the silence, she'd felt herself about to cry. And knew for a moment that, if he couldn't reach her, she wanted to be as separate from this man as it was possible to be. With him, she was isolated.

After she put the phone down, she coaxed two cups of tea from the machine and walked back up the worn central dip in the stone staircase. Along the first floor corridors, she tried not to look into the little cubicles, for fear of intruding on others' distress, or having it intrude upon her. Perhaps if one of them were ill, she or Alan, it would be different.

When she got to the door at the end, she placed one of the paper cups on a little table piled high with disposable bedpans and knocked, gently. She felt she should knock.

The voice inside was quiet, distracted. As she manoeuvred in with the cups, Patsy saw that Evie might have fallen asleep for a moment. She now made haste to smooth down her hair, straightening the tucks in her blouse.

Tea? said Patsy, redundantly. Thank you, darling, said Evie. I'll bring it round, said Patsy, skirting the foot of the bed. Where shall I put it? On the windowsill – can you reach it there?

Evie moved her chair a little so her right hand could reach out to the paper cup. The two smiled at the awkwardness of the movement. She sipped a little and Patsy took the cup from her and placed it on the sill.

Evie turned back to the bed where her left hand held Donald's. The last stroke had drained the power from his right side, the remaining good side. He lay now, curled on the bed, his crinkly hair fanned out and white. Oh, your nails, tutted Evie, how did you let them get so long? It's terrible, she said, chuckling. Let me find my little scissors.

Patsy felt a slight embarrassment. Perhaps she should leave them alone for this ritual? Evie had bent over Donald's shoulder, her arm curving around his neck. She was whispering into his ear, as if he were sleeping out on a meadow somewhere and she had just tiptoed up to surprise him. A short moan burst into the room. Patsy was surprised by its strength, but then he was a big man. It alarmed her, too: was he distressed, or angry? Evie rocked back a little, smiling, running a hand over the wild hair in admiration, as if he'd just uttered a complex witticism.

Patsy had visited two or three times since they'd been back. Sally cycled from the new house from time to time to see Evie at home, but they'd agreed the hospital might be too upsetting. Until recently, Patsy hadn't seen the couple for more than a year, just after Donald's first stroke, when she'd returned to England to talk to agents about selling the house and finding something better.

Then, in a dark little nursing home overshadowed by pines, Donald had still been able to talk, although with difficulty. He'd been effervescent that afternoon, pressing the emergency bell by the oxygen mask every couple of minutes to order more champagne. They're so good, the nurses, confided Evie, they don't mind, they just ignore it. Although sometimes they bring him a little fizzy apple juice. And well, we enjoy it – don't we, darling?

Donald was on the Côte d'Azur, or had pulled into the little hotel at Ravello. He'd showered after the day's drive and changed into cream slacks and a fresh white shirt. From the balcony, he could look down on the business of the street or the little port, enjoying his cigarette while Evie worked magic in the bathroom, conjuring bottles and creams from her snakeskin case. He picked up the phone and pressed the button for room service. Later, they'd find that restaurant the doorman had pointed out. For now, a glass or two of champagne, and the panoramic vista of darkening sea, twinkling lights and, at the end of the hundred and eighty degree turn, his wife's legs beneath the lacy slip.

From the doorway, Patsy gave a little wave, childlike. Bye now. As before, she felt she'd been intruding. Evie acknowledged the wave with a smile and a tilt of her head; both her hands were massaging Donald's liver-spotted claws, the large tanned hands that Patsy remembered reaching across the keyboard of the baby grand. Bye, darling, she whispered in her throaty drawl, thank you for coming: we have enjoyed it. Haven't we, my love? she said, bending into his shoulder once more, relaxing back into the comfort of his company.

There are great ideas out there that never really had their moment, stymied by cartels and politics and internal feuds or simple bad timing. For all he has benefited from the power of large corporations, Alan still treasures his Betamax player, wishes he could have driven an electric car in the fifties and subscribes enthusiastically to idealistic computer communities that have no truck with the Microsoft empire. He still believes in the egalitarian desirability of a wash'n'wear suit.

When he allows himself the indulgence of hindsight, Alan can't help but see those early years of the 1960s as a peculiarly blessed time. It is then, he reckons (although this is a heresy he must conceal from his life partner of the last twenty years), that he was most himself. There was something particularly open and promising, too, about Patsy when she first joined him in America – a vulnerability that slipped away. But at that moment it was almost magnificent, the two of them, Alan and Patsy, setting off together with their little family on their American adventure.

He couldn't grasp it at the time, but it was a Golden Age.

16

INSIDE THE window, it is hot. A pair of bluebottles lie on the metal sill. Grey streaks run down the glass. Jimmy's nose lies between the dusty tramlines, squashed against the pane. This time, this time, he gets to go through the magic gateway.

They've been at the airport for nearly an hour. A combination of his mother and Mr Rookin and the two huge cars from the taxi service has delivered the family comfortably ahead of schedule. Jimmy doesn't mind. He's going to be a pilot. Well, probably. It's useful observation time, in any case.

They're all dressed up; the girls have matching dresses with smocked panels and white cardigans, which makes Lucy really mad. Evie helped them all get ready this morning. They stayed overnight in the spare room at Evie and Donald's. Everything was all packed up at home and some special cleaners are coming in today. Mummy says it's too depressing at home now. Jimmy's wearing his suit, but with the short trousers: it was sweltering even when they left home. Sally is kicking her white shoes against the leg of her mother's chair. Lucy is staring at her book. Jimmy doesn't think she's reading. Lucy can be so wet.

There were so many tears. Evie wouldn't let go of Sally, kissing her all over the face. She had this little handkerchief held to her mouth. Donald pushed half a crown into his hand and pretended to cuff his ear. *He* didn't cry: in fact, he hardly said anything at all, except he picked Mum up and swung her around, as though he were a young man. And whispered something in her ear. Then she began to cry, too.

In the departure lounge Patsy is looking around at them, bright-eyed. Her suit is pale blue – I like the colour, Mum, Jimmy had said, struck by her perfection. Then she had to spoil it, embarrassing him with a hug like a boa constrictor. Thank you, darling, thank you. Do you think Daddy will like it?

She's been talking about Daddy all the time this past week. All the things they're going to do – the swimming and the holidays, how she plans to have a barbecue at least once a week, and drive-in movies, and holidays in the national parks. She has a folder of leaflets from the tourist office or something, which she is actually bringing with her. As if the Americans didn't know about their own country. Jimmy is reacting less and less to the plans; it's almost painful to contemplate the menu of riches. He feels like saying, don't go on about it. It won't be perfect, it can't be that good. The roof will leak or something. He hates it when she's like this.

In her mind's eye, Patsy has started on the kitchen. Alan has sent some photographs of the house – they're not good ones, but they give some clue about the colours anyway. And there's nothing that can't be changed, no fault in a room that can't be improved in some way by imaginative rearrangement of the furniture. Or the addition of a spectacular feature to draw attention from an ugly fault.

Jimmy has been sent over to the tea bar. Yes, they can have drinks and crisps if they don't get salt everywhere. The woman behind the counter has a gap in her teeth when she smiles at him and takes his half-crown. The radio behind her on the red Formica shelf crackles out the lunchtime request programme.

Twenty-four hours from Tulse Hill, sings Jimmy to the others as he carries the tray to the little wood-effect table. No, Jimmy, says his mother, sharply. Stop that. Stop it. She sounds as though she might shriek. It is *not* Tulse Hill. But you're less than twenty-four hours away from Daddy, he protests. You don't have to worry any more. The girls look at him. Shut up, say Lucy's eyes. Shut up.

Or maybe he doesn't sing that. Maybe he does that on another occasion. Maybe his mother shouts at him later, when they're already in America. Perhaps the song on the airport radio is another nasal lament, Brenda Lee or someone. He's thought about this and though he knows it's impossible – the record won't be made for another year or two – whenever he hears Pitney he thinks of that departure lounge and Lucy's look, as her eyes rise defensively from the book.

I hate to do this to you.

Beyond the gate is the best chance of the best future they could ever dream. Good income, good prospects; it's all going to be fine, Patsy tells herself. You know, half the time she just can't work out what she and Alan ever disagree about. It all seems so silly now and when she sees him, at last, all the old problems will melt away. Leave it all behind. They'll be able to talk, properly, spend time together. Fall in love.

But I love somebody new.

What can, I do?

That's it, cries Jimmy. That was the call, let's go. The girls scramble for their little bags. Quick, Mummy, quick. Patsy smiles wide at them all. Here we go, then. Come on, darlings. Let's go to see Daddy.

Patsy picks up her handbag and her vanity case and takes Sally with her free hand. She shifts her weight slightly on to one hip, straightens the lining in her skirt, checks her seams and leads the children through the gateway.

Acknowledgments

Thanks to Brian Aldiss for pointing me in the direction of vintage futurology, to Dr David Hinks at the College of Textiles in North Carolina and Dr David Giachardi of the Royal Society of Chemistry in London, to Jef McAllister, London Bureau Chief of *Time* for access to archives and Jackie Schlesinger in Raleigh for home movies and hospitality, to my agent Clare Alexander and, once again, to Alison Samuel for her clarity and encouragement. And thanks also to Robert Lance Hughes, who was compelled by me to draw beneath his competence.